Enid's right, Elizabeth reflected. *It* is *as if everyone who works here took some kind of magic beauty pill.* She started to think about the unusually young and attractive employees, and the strange rule about not leaving the grounds that Chris had told her applied to all staff members, every day of the week—even when they weren't working. She pictured Katya's sad eyes and recalled the remark about her mother that hinted somehow at sorrow or loss. Suddenly Elizabeth shivered, despite the balmy air wafting through the open window. For a brief moment the enchantment of her evening with Chris faded, leaving her with a vague feeling of foreboding. Paradise Spa was a beautiful, magical place . . . wasn't it? Or was it possible that all wasn't quite as perfect as it seemed?

MURDER IN PARADISE

Written by
Kate William

Created by
FRANCINE PASCAL

BANTAM BOOKS
NEW YORK • TORONTO • LONDON • SYDNEY • AUCKLAND

RL 6, age 12 and up

MURDER IN PARADISE
A Bantam Book / April 1995

Sweet Valley High® is a registered trademark of Francine Pascal
Conceived by Francine Pascal
Produced by Daniel Weiss Associates, Inc.
33 West 17th Street
New York, NY 10011
Cover art by Bruce Emmett

ISBN: 0-553-56710-1

Published simultaneously in the United States and Canada

Bantam Books are published by Bantam Books, a division of Bantam Doubleday Dell Publishing Group, Inc. Its trademark, consisting of the words "Bantam Books" and the portrayal of a rooster, is Registered in U.S. Patent and Trademark Office and in other countries. Marca Registrada. Bantam Books, 1540 Broadway, New York, New York 10036.

PRINTED IN THE UNITED STATES OF AMERICA

OPM 0 9 8 7 6 5 4 3 2 1

To Billy Carmen

Chapter 1

"I can't believe we're on our way to the most luxurious spa in all of California!" enthused sixteen-year-old Jessica Wakefield, her blue-green eyes sparkling with anticipation.

The train was racing up the coast; every minute brought them closer to the fabled Paradise Spa. Hardly able to contain her excitement, Jessica bounced up and down as she looked out her window at the dramatic view of ocean and cliffs. "For a whole week of being pampered and beautified. No homework, no cooking dinner or washing dishes . . ."

"Like you ever do those things," kidded her identical twin sister, Elizabeth.

Mrs. Wakefield laughed. "I guess there's one thing we're not leaving behind," she observed. "You two teasing each other!"

Pushing a strand of bright-blond hair off her forehead, Elizabeth smiled fondly at her mother. "You're so nice to take us along on this trip, Mom," she said. "You could have *really* gotten away from it all and left us at home! But I'm glad you didn't. This is the most incredible treat."

"It really is, Alice," agreed Grace Fowler, the elegant and attractive mother of Jessica's best friend, Lila.

Alice Wakefield gave Elizabeth's hand a squeeze. "Well, I thought about it carefully, and if I may say so, I came up with the perfect group to share my free spa vacation with. A mother-daughter getaway seemed like a natural. Think about it, Liz. Can you imagine your father or Steven enjoying facials and mud packs?"

Elizabeth burst out laughing as she pictured her handsome attorney father and college-aged brother in matching terry-cloth robes and turbans getting their toenails painted. "You've got a point," she agreed. She turned to Enid Rollins, who was sitting on the other side of her. "This is going to be so much fun. I'm so glad you could come, too, Enid!"

Enid smiled. "So am I."

When Alice Wakefield learned she'd won an all-expenses-paid week at Paradise Spa for herself and six guests, she'd invited Lila and Grace Fowler and Enid and Adele Rollins in addition to her own two daughters. Enid's mother was the only one who hadn't been able to take the time off.

"Paradise Spa." Jessica let the delicious syllables roll off her tongue. "Doesn't it sound like the kind of place where dreams come true?"

Lila sighed rapturously. She, too, savored the words. "Paradise Spa. Celebrities go there all the time. And now it's our turn!"

Jessica opened the glossy brochure that she held in her lap; Lila leaned close to look over her shoulder at the pictures. "The buildings are fabulous," Lila gushed. "It looks like a Renaissance villa in the Italian countryside."

Jessica pointed to a photo. "Look at these mineral pools!"

"And the exercise room," said Lila. "All the most state-of-the-art equipment."

"Even the food looks good," said Jessica, examining the picture of a buffet table in a flower-filled open-air dining room.

"We're going to be busy, that's for sure," commented Lila as she read from the list of beauty and relaxation treatments and athletic activities offered at the spa. "Swedish massage, aromatherapy, steam bath, facial and full-body mud packs, yoga, golf, tennis . . . And listen to this." Turning back to the owner's note on the first page, Lila read it aloud to the others. "'It is my firm and passionate belief that inside everyone, no matter how plain, a beautiful person waits to be discovered. Here at Paradise Spa, I make that my personal mission: Surrounding my clients with beauty and comfort, I encourage the beautiful person within each of them to blossom forth. Yours in beauty, Tatiana Mueller.' "

"Wow," breathed Jessica, her eyes starry. "If she can do all that for *ugly* people, just think what *we'll* look like when she's finished with us!"

"We'll be ravishing," Lila agreed, tossing her long, wavy brown hair.

"Goddesses," Jessica predicted.

Elizabeth looked at Enid and shook her head, laughing. Even after sixteen years her sister's vanity sometimes amazed her. Undeniably, the Wakefield twins had been blessed with all-American beauty: silky golden hair, sparkling long-lashed eyes the color of the Pacific Ocean, and suntanned slender bodies, thanks to their active southern-California lifestyles. But while Jessica made the most of her natural advantages, favoring trendy, skimpy fashions, subtle but sexy makeup, and glamorous hairstyles, Elizabeth tended to play down her looks. She was most comfortable in khaki shorts and a polo shirt, with her long blond hair pulled back in a barrette or ponytail. Maybe that was because Elizabeth thought who a person was inside and what she did was more important than how she looked. She was serious about her schoolwork and put her whole heart and soul into the writing she did for the Sweet Valley High newspaper, *The Oracle*. In contrast to Jessica, who enjoyed attracting boys by the dozen like bees to honey, Elizabeth was content with the admiration and affection of one special guy, her longtime boyfriend, Todd Wilkins.

Jessica knew Elizabeth thought she was self-centered and shallow because she was more interested in sorority activities and cheerleading than earning honor-roll grades, and given a choice, she'd take the beach or the mall over the library any day. She couldn't care less. She voiced her thoughts out loud. "Someday, Liz, when you're old and gray and no man will look twice at you anymore, you'll think back on this trip and kick yourself for not making the most of what Paradise Spa has to offer."

Elizabeth just laughed. "I guess we expect different things from it."

"OK," conceded Jessica. "What's *your* goal, if it's not to become irresistibly gorgeous?"

"I just want a quiet, peaceful week of girl talk and healthy living," Elizabeth replied. "And I brought my new laptop with me, in case I feel inspired to do some writing."

Jessica groaned and rolled her eyes. "You're bringing your *computer* to a *spa*? I'm sure Tatiana Mueller has rules against things like that!"

Elizabeth folded her arms across her chest. "So I'm supposed to spend my spare time gawking at celebrities and scoping the place for cute guys?"

Jessica dimpled mischievously. "Sure!"

"I'm with Jessica," drawled Lila, stretching her

long, slender legs and reclining in her seat. "I don't know how you can even think about *working* on this vacation, Liz. I'm not going to lift a finger the whole week—I want to be waited on hand and foot."

"Big change that's going to be," teased Jessica.

As the daughter of one of the wealthiest and most successful computer-industry magnates in the country, Lila lived in a palatial home in Sweet Valley, complete with tennis court, swimming pool, and full-time servants. Her walletful of charge cards with unlimited credit was a constant source of envy for Jessica, who was always begging for an advance on her allowance to pay for impulsive shopping purchases.

Lila grinned. "True. But we don't have a masseuse on staff at Fowler Crest. Not yet, anyway!"

Elizabeth caught her mother's eye, and they exchanged a smile. "What about you, Mom?" Elizabeth asked. "Do you want Tatiana Mueller to encourage the beautiful person inside you to come to the surface?"

Mrs. Wakefield, who was often mistaken for the older sister of the twins, chuckled. "I imagine I'll look about the same when the week's over, and that's fine with me. My main object is to have some quality time with you girls."

"Same goes for me," declared Mrs. Fowler. "I'm just happy to have this special time with Li."

"And all because Mom got her name picked at random out of the phone book!" exclaimed Jessica.

Mrs. Wakefield shook her head, smiling. "Isn't it funny? Sometimes when you least expect it, life hands you the most wonderful surprise!"

Elizabeth couldn't help noticing that her best friend remained oddly pensive and silent while the others cheerfully discussed their expectations for the week at Paradise Spa. When she and Enid took a walk to the club car to buy a soda and a snack, Elizabeth asked Enid what was on her mind.

Pushing back her curly auburn hair, Enid heaved a melancholy sigh. "I was really disappointed when Mom decided at the last minute that she couldn't come with us to Paradise. I mean, of course I understand—she has a ton of work—but it's still a letdown. Mostly, though, it's Hugh," she admitted. She bit her lip; Elizabeth could tell she was fighting back tears. "I still can't believe he broke up with me. I thought everything between us was fine. Boy, was I living in a fantasy world!"

Elizabeth patted her friend's arm sympathetically. "You two went out for a long time, and I know you really cared about him. But even though it may take a while, you'll get over him. I promise."

Enid didn't look convinced. "I just feel so . . . crummy," she confessed. "I feel ugly and boring and—" They were standing at the snack counter. She started to reach for a bag of potato chips, then drew her hand back. "And *fat*."

"You're *not* fat," Elizabeth protested.

"I am too," countered Enid morosely. "I've gained four pounds since Hugh dumped me."

Elizabeth paid for two diet sodas and then deftly steered Enid away from the snacks. They sat down at a table by the window. "Look," Elizabeth said in her firmest, most upbeat tone. She pulled the paper wrapper from a straw, then stuck the straw into the soda can. "You can't let the fact that Hugh broke up with you make you feel bad about yourself. You're the same person you've always been."

"Right," said Enid glumly. "That's what's so depressing. I'm the same old dull, plain, ordinary Enid. Only now I don't even have a boyfriend, and I'll probably never be asked out on another date for as long as I live!"

"Enid!" exclaimed Elizabeth. "That's the most ridiculous thing I've ever heard you say."

"It's not ridiculous, it's true," insisted Enid. "Hugh told me he didn't want to be tied down. You know what *that* means. He wants to date other girls. I'm just positive that if I were prettier . . ." Her green eyes glittered; a tear slid down her freckled cheek. "If I were prettier, if I looked more like you and Jessica, Hugh would never have gotten tired of me."

Elizabeth continued to shake her head emphatically. Inside, though, she had to admit that there might be a tiny measure of truth to what Enid said. Right after breaking up with Enid, Hugh had asked out a dim-brained but extremely cute and curvy Sweet Valley High sophomore named Sabrina. It really did seem as if he were going for superficial sex appeal over substance.

Elizabeth didn't intend to remind Enid about Sabrina, however. Her role was to boost her friend's confidence, and in that department Elizabeth knew she was as good a cheerleader as Jessica. "You *are* pretty," Elizabeth told Enid firmly and sincerely, "and you don't need some guy to prove it to you. None of us should need guys to make us feel attractive, and that's why this is going to be such a great week. It will be just us girls, spoiling ourselves rotten."

Enid cracked a weak smile. "I guess that sounds OK. I'd be happy if I never laid eyes on another male person of masculine persuasion."

Elizabeth laughed. "That's the spirit, Enid," she cheered. "You need a change of scenery and routine, that's all. Tatiana Mueller and I guarantee that Paradise Spa will be the perfect cure for a broken heart!"

Saturday was more than half over when they arrived at tiny Paradise Station. Jessica was so eager to disembark that she jumped to her feet while the train was still moving. "We're here!"

Its brakes squealing, the train rolled to a stop. Gazing out the window, Jessica spotted a white van with kelly-green and magenta lettering parked in the lot adjacent to the tracks. "Paradise Spa sent a van for us," she informed the others. "Wow, they really do things in style."

Then something else interesting caught her eye . . . or, rather, some*one*. An incredibly handsome boy with jet-black hair and light-blue eyes was standing on the platform gazing expectantly at the newly arrived train. A crisp white polo and matching shorts showcased his golden-bronze tan and tall, well-muscled body. It was all Jessica could do to keep from licking her lips.

"Whoa, don't look now," she exclaimed, "but I think I'm falling in love!"

Suitcase in hand, Elizabeth stepped up behind her sister. "Aren't you already in love?" she asked Jessica. "Don't tell me you've forgotten Ken already."

"Ken who?" Jessica joked. Of course she hadn't forgotten about Ken Matthews, Sweet Valley High's star quarterback and her own current boyfriend. But she was on vacation, for heaven's sake. Wasn't Elizabeth going to let her have any fun?

When the door slid open, Jessica was the first to hop onto the platform. The black-haired boy walked toward her, a welcoming smile on his movie-star handsome face. With delight Jessica read the words embroidered in kelly green on his polo shirt: PARADISE SPA STAFF. *This is my lucky day!* she thought gleefully.

The boy lifted his hand in a cheerful wave. "I'm Chris," he said, smiling broadly at the whole group, "and Mrs. Mueller sent me to drive you to Paradise

Spa." Chris took the suitcase from Elizabeth's hand, then reached for the bag Mrs. Fowler was carrying. "Now, you all just wait right here while I load the luggage into the van. It'll only take a minute."

Jessica didn't mind waiting . . . and watching Chris's biceps ripple as he hoisted the suitcases. She noticed that despite her "What about Ken?" remark, Elizabeth, too, had been struck dumb by Chris's extraordinary good looks. "Don't tell me you've forgotten Todd *already*," Jessica whispered maliciously into her sister's ear; Elizabeth flushed crimson.

A few minutes later the twins, their mother, Lila, Mrs. Fowler, and Enid were all comfortably seated in the luxurious van. Hopping into the driver's seat, Chris started the engine. "This is a spectacular drive," he said, turning to glance over his shoulder at Elizabeth, "so sit back and enjoy the ride."

Jessica, who'd snagged the front passenger seat, buckled her seat belt. The van rolled forward. The final leg of their journey had begun—they were almost to their destination!

There was no town to speak of at Paradise Station—just an old-fashioned general store that did triple duty as a gas station and post office. Almost immediately they'd left all signs of civilization behind. They were driving into the coastal hills; the narrow road twisted and climbed. Lush vegetation—palm fronds and exotic flowering shrubs—pressed close on either side.

"So, Chris," Jessica said, fluttering her eyelashes at him, "tell us about Paradise Spa. Is it really as wonderful as it looks in the brochure?"

"It's a magical place, all right," he affirmed breezily. "I promise, when your week is up, if you're like most satisfied Paradise Spa clients, you won't want to go home again."

No, I definitely won't, thought Jessica, drinking in the rugged lines of his profile, *if things go my way and you and I fall madly in love with each other!*

She was already plotting how to spend as much time as possible with Chris the adorable chauffeur. "So this is your job?" she asked. "Driving guests to and from the station?"

"That's part of my job," he replied. "I'm also the golf pro. Do you golf?"

Jessica considered golf the most boring sport on earth . . . until this moment. "No, but I'm *dying* to learn," she told Chris, ignoring Elizabeth's "hmph" from the backseat.

Chris just smiled, whistling a lighthearted tune as he steered the van deeper and deeper into the forest. Jessica gazed out at the junglelike greenery. *I can't believe I'm still in California,* she thought, watching a pair of brilliantly plumed birds dart through the trees. *This is like another planet, a fantasyland.*

The van rounded a bend in the road. Up ahead Jessica caught a glimpse of the low vine-covered spa buildings—she recognized them from the picture in the brochure. A delicious shiver of anticipation chased up her spine. The dream vacation was about to commence. What kind of adventures were in store for the six of them in Paradise?

Chris parked the van under a portico in front of the entrance to the main building. Jessica, Elizabeth, and the rest of the Sweet Valley group stepped out into the balmy late afternoon.

The buildings were surrounded by lush greenery and a rainbow of flowers. Alice Wakefield drew in a deep breath. "Umm—I smell the ocean, and some absolutely heavenly roses," she said with a blissful smile. "I can feel the tension melting out of my body already."

Two porters materialized, and in seconds all the luggage was quietly whisked out of sight. Jessica jabbed Lila hard with her elbow. "Li, did you *see* those guys?" she whispered, still gawking after them. "I swear, they were as gorgeous as Chris. Could that be *possible*?"

Just then a group of people in Paradise Spa T-shirts jogged by, led by a tall, svelte young woman with a cascading golden ponytail. The young woman was cheering on the others, many of whom were huffing and puffing from the exertion; meanwhile, she was smiling cheerfully, not winded in the least.

Jessica took note of the girl's classical features: the high cheekbones and ruler-straight nose, the gracefully arched eyebrows, wide-set eyes, and full lips. "I don't think I've ever seen anyone that beautiful," Jessica said, awestruck by the girl's physical perfection.

"She looks like a statue," Lila agreed. "Diana or Venus or somebody. She doesn't look *real*."

Elizabeth, Enid, Mrs. Wakefield, and Mrs. Fowler had entered the lobby; Jessica and Lila followed suit. They all paused just inside the door to admire the simple elegance of the lobby, which was decorated with fresh flowers and greens, hardwood floors and beams, mission-style furniture, and simple flowing white drapes at the floor-to-ceiling windows that opened out onto a sunny courtyard. Staff members in crisp, sporty uniforms bustled about.

"Am I seeing things, or does everyone who works here, from the receptionist to the gardeners, look like a model?" asked Elizabeth.

"Mrs. Mueller wasn't kidding about the effects of this place," Jessica agreed.

"I wonder what *she'll* look like," mused Lila.

"With a romantic name like Tatiana, I bet she'll be the most beautiful of all," Elizabeth predicted.

"I feel like a toad," muttered Enid.

At that moment Jessica spied a woman in a spotless white lab coat scurrying toward them. "Speaking of toads," Jessica hissed. So much for the theory that everyone employed by Paradise Spa was beautiful!

The woman was about their mother's age and height, but any resemblance to Alice Wakefield ended there. Her frizzy reddish hair was streaked with gray and her skin was sallow; her nose looked crooked and she had no chin to speak of; her body was as dumpy and lumpy as a sack of potatoes.

When the woman drew closer, however, a blush of shame stained Jessica's cheeks, and immediately she wished she could retract her offhandedly cruel remark. Now she could see that one side of the woman's face was scarred and disfigured, as if she'd been in a terrible accident.

The woman walked right up to Jessica, her hand extended. Jessica read the name tag pinned to the lab coat, and her jaw dropped. *This* homely creature was the celebrated Tatiana Mueller?

Mrs. Mueller grasped Jessica's limp hand and squeezed it tightly. "Welcome, welcome to Paradise, my lovelies!" she chirped, turning next to Elizabeth. "Twins, my goodness. And what *beautiful* twins." Mrs. Mueller patted Elizabeth on the arm. "And their mother!" Now Mrs. Mueller was staring at Alice, a rapt expression on her lopsided face. "The template of loveliness. You must be Alice Wakefield."

"Yes, I am."

Mrs. Mueller took Alice's hand. "Such a pleasure to welcome you, our special prizewinner."

"It's a pleasure to be here," Mrs. Wakefield replied.

Meanwhile, Lila was whispering into Jessica's ear. "The template of loveliness? What the heck does that mean?" Jessica stifled a giggle.

"Now, my dears," continued Mrs. Mueller, smiling warmly at Grace Fowler, "my only rule while you are here is this: Think only beautiful thoughts!" She beckoned. "Come, come, let me show you to your rooms."

Turning, Mrs. Mueller strode with swift, light steps down the hall. The Sweet Valley group hurried after her.

Jessica rolled her eyes for her mother's benefit. "Can you believe this lady?" she whispered. "All that corny 'my lovelies' business?"

"Well, you *are* lovely, honey." A bemused look crossed Alice's face as she gazed after their hostess. "You know, I feel like I've met Mrs. Mueller before," she murmured, wrinkling her forehead.

"Really?" said Jessica. "Where? When?"

Mrs. Wakefield thought for a moment, then shook her head. "I don't remember."

"Mom," said Jessica, "don't you think you'd remember meeting someone like Tatiana Mueller? I mean, she's . . . *unusual*, to put it mildly."

Mrs. Wakefield smiled. "You're probably right. It must be my imagination."

Having left the main building, they walked along a path that wound through a cluster of picturesque redwood cottages. "I've put you in Tranquillity Cottage," said Mrs. Mueller, taking a key ring from her pocket. "There are three bedrooms, each with a private bath and a common living area." She unlocked the door, then handed out keys. "I hope you'll be comfortable here."

Jessica entered the cottage eagerly. "It's beautiful!" she gushed, rushing over to stick her nose into an enormous bouquet of exotic white flowers. She popped her head into each of the three bedrooms, then peeked out onto the deck. "Our very own hot tub!"

"Our luggage is already in the rooms," observed Elizabeth. "Look, Enid. You and I have this adorable room with the fluffy goose-down comforter and watercolor paintings!"

Lila's and Jessica's suitcases were placed in the bedroom next to Elizabeth and Enid's. "We have a window seat," Lila called to Jessica, "and a sunken tub!"

Alice and Grace were sharing the third bedroom. "Ours is the most beautiful of all," exclaimed Mrs. Wakefield. "A handmade quilt and dozens of pillows, candles in sconces on the wall, a writing desk and a daybed for relaxing with a book, fresh flowers everywhere . . ."

"Heaven," said Grace.

Alice smiled. *"Paradise,"* she corrected.

Mrs. Mueller had hovered in the living room, enjoying their reactions. Now she waved a hand before slipping through the door. "Get settled, my dears," she urged, "and then might I suggest a refreshing swim before you join the rest of the guests in the alfresco dining area?"

Five minutes later they'd all changed into bathing suits. Donning one of the plush terry-cloth robes that was hanging in her closet, Jessica padded in bare feet to the swimming pool. Night was falling, and Japanese lanterns cast a festive glow on the water; the intoxicating scent of hibiscus filled the evening air.

They had the pool to themselves. "It *is* Paradise," Jessica said to Elizabeth as she slipped off her robe and waded into the cool water. "Don't you think this is the most beautiful place in the world?"

Elizabeth nodded in complete agreement. "This is going to be a week we'll never forget."

Lila stood poised on the edge of the pool. "Remember, ladies!" she called out before diving in. "Only beautiful thoughts!"

"This is strange. This is very strange," said

Jessica a minute after stepping out of the shower.

They'd returned from their swim and were getting ready for dinner. After toweling herself off in the bathroom, she'd turned to face the mirror over the sink . . . only to realize for the first time that there was no mirror.

She opened the medicine cabinet; no mirror there. Nor was there a mirror on the back of the bathroom door.

"What's strange?" asked Lila when Jessica returned to the bedroom.

"There's no mirror in there," Jessica informed her as she ran a comb through her wet hair. "And look—there isn't one in here, either!"

It was true. There were sconces on the walls, and original artwork in gilded frames, but no looking glass of any size, shape, or style. "Hmm. Maybe in the living room," suggested Lila.

"Nope," called Jessica after scouting out the living room. "Well, I'll just have to borrow Liz's. How else am I going to make sure I'm as absolutely beautiful as I can be, in case I run into Chris at dinner?"

She knocked on her sister's door and was crestfallen to learn that they, too, had no mirror in their room. Running across the hall to her mother's room, she asked Alice and Grace the same question. "Do you guys have a mirror?"

A quick check revealed no mirror there, either.

"There's not a single mirror in the entire cottage!" Jessica concluded, mystified.

Already dressed in a pair of black silk palazzo pants and a fuchsia silk tank top, Lila was busily applying her makeup. "I've done this so many millions of times, I don't need a mirror," she said as she dabbed at her long eyelashes with a mascara brush. "And you don't need a mirror, either. I'll tell you which outfit to wear."

"OK," said Jessica with a disgruntled sigh. She held up two choices. "The linen pants and jacket with a silk tank, or the orange dress. Sophisticated or sexy."

"I'd think it would be obvious," remarked Lila. "You want to catch this guy's eye? Go with the low neck and the high hemline!"

Obediently, Jessica put on the burnt-orange raw-silk dress. It fit like a glove, and she knew she looked great in it, but without the confirmation of a good, long look in a mirror, she felt naked and insecure. "Are you sure this is OK?" she fussed. "What about jewelry? And which shoes?"

Lila pulled a compact out of her purse and tossed it at Jessica. "Here. Try this."

The compact wasn't much help. Jessica could see only a tiny part of herself at a time: her face, her neck, her knees. "Oh, I can't go to the dining room looking like this!" she wailed.

"You look fine," Lila snapped impatiently. "Geez, Jess, get a grip. I can't believe you're in such a tizzy over one of Mrs. Mueller's *employees*."

"An unbelievably *cute* employee," Jessica reminded Lila as she tried to make out her reflection in the sliding glass door. "They're all cute, and I want them to notice me!"

"You can have them," declared Lila, spritzing her throat with perfume. "I'm setting my sights a little higher. One of the other guests, maybe—a wealthy bachelor type."

"Well, good luck, looking like that," smirked Jessica. She tossed the compact back to Lila. "You have lipstick all over your teeth!"

As she got ready for dinner, Elizabeth was glad she wasn't sharing a room with her sister. Jessica would immediately have accused her of primping in hopes of running into Chris . . . and she would have been right.

He wasn't that cute, Elizabeth tried unsuccessfully to convince herself as she brushed her hair back on one side and clipped it with a silver-and-turquoise barrette. *I mean, he's cute, but Todd's cuter. I'm not interested in meeting guys at Paradise Spa—I already have a boyfriend. Besides, Jess saw Chris first, so by rights he's hers.*

All this reasoning didn't change the fact that Elizabeth couldn't get Chris out of her mind. He *was* cute—he was more than cute. He had the kind of face you saw once and never forgot. *And those eyes,* thought Elizabeth dreamily, *and that smile . . . the way he looked at me . . .*

Feeling incredibly guilty, she took her laptop computer from its carrying case and plugged it in. Disconnecting the phone line, she plugged that into the back of her computer. The computer was brand new and she was still learning how to use it, but she knew how to do a few things, such as log on and send an E-mail message to Todd, who had a personal computer and modem at home.

Elizabeth typed in her password and Todd's E-mail address, then began writing her message. "Dear Todd," she typed. "Paradise Spa is wonderful. Our rooms are beautiful, and we just took a swim in one of the mineral pools—already I feel totally relaxed. After dinner we'll have a tour of the facilities, and tomorrow we start our personal beauty and fitness regimens. You may not recognize me when I get back! Just kidding. Wish you were here. Lots of love and kisses . . ."

Elizabeth signed off. Writing to Todd made her feel close to him for a moment, but as soon as she turned her back on the computer screen, thoughts of another boy elbowed their way into her imagination.

Just then Enid emerged from the bathroom, dressed for dinner in a white skirt and pink blouse. "Ready to go, Liz?" she asked.

Elizabeth jumped to her feet and practically sprinted to the door. "Am I ever!"

They strolled to the dining room with the rest of their party. As the balmy evening breeze lifted the hair off her neck, Enid felt herself shiver with nervous anticipation. At dinner they'd be meeting some of the other guests. Often she felt shy in situations like this. *Luckily I have Liz to hide behind,* Enid thought.

The group breezed into the open-air dining room and were immediately seated at a table for six. Watching the other guests out of the corner of her eye, Enid noticed that many of them were spectacularly glamorous—hardly in need of diets and beauty treatments, as far as she could tell! She also noticed that quite a few heads turned in the direction of the Sweet Valley party . . . or, rather, in the direction of the twins and their mother, and Lila and Mrs. Fowler. *Everybody's thinking "What beautiful mothers and daughters,"* Enid supposed, hunching her shoulders and dropping her chin to her chest. *Nobody's taking a second look at me.*

Slinking to her chair, she dropped into it with relief. "Did you see?" Jessica was whispering excitedly. "At the table across the room? I could swear it's . . ." She named a famous older movie actress.

Lila swiveled in her seat to see. "It *is* her," she confirmed.

"I always wondered what the secret to her ageless beauty was," said Grace, "and now I know. It's a stay at Paradise Spa!"

A plate of fresh greens with oil-free vinaigrette dressing was placed before each of them by a pretty young waitress named Lulu with chic cropped brown hair; she reminded Enid of the cover girl on that month's issue of *Teen Scene.*

Enid picked without much appetite at her salad, feeling more like an ugly duckling than ever. *Even the kitchen staff is drop-dead gorgeous. There's no doubt about it—I'm the least attractive person at the whole spa!*

Jessica was also uninterested in her salad, but for a different reason. "Look!" she whispered excitedly. "There's Chris!"

Sure enough, the spa's golf pro and chauffeur was sauntering toward their table. Jessica flashed him her most dazzling smile; Enid noticed that Elizabeth, too, looked especially animated all of a sudden.

"It's nice to see you again, ladies," Chris greeted them gallantly. "How do you like Paradise Spa so far?"

"Oh, everything's just perfect—divine," Jessica gushed. "There are so many things to do and I want to do them all, starting with golf."

"Really?" Chris raised his eyebrows, smiling. "So I'll see you out on the course tomorrow?"

"Actually, I'd like to sign up for a private lesson. I'm a beginner and I'll need *lots* of special attention," Jessica said meaningfully.

"Paradise Spa will be happy to accommodate you," said Chris. "I'm free at nine. How about the rest of you? Is anyone else interested in learning how to putt and drive?"

Chris looked straight at Elizabeth with an encouraging smile. Enid saw Elizabeth open her mouth as if to reply but then grimace and shake her head instead.

"You didn't have to do that," Elizabeth grumbled to Jessica after Chris walked away. She reached down to rub the foot that Jessica had stomped on. "I wasn't going to horn in on your date."

"Just making sure," Jessica said breezily.

"Golf lessons." Lila snorted. "Really, Jessica. Are you that desperate?"

Jessica arched her eyebrows at Lila. "I don't see you having any luck snagging that wealthy bachelor you were fantasizing about," she retorted.

"That's because I haven't spotted him yet," Lila drawled. Then her eyes widened. "Or maybe I spoke too soon. Look over there, the table behind the potted palm tree!"

They all turned to look, Enid included, in time to see a man in dark glasses who'd been dining alone pat his mouth with his napkin, rise, and leave the dining room. "Did you see him?" Lila squealed. "That profile—that hair—the cut of his suit! It's him!"

"Who?" asked Jessica.

"I don't know exactly," admitted Lila, "but I'm sure he's someone rich and famous . . . and single." She smiled confidently. "And I have a whole week to get to know him!"

The rest of the meal—poached salmon with a

light dill sauce, haricots verts, steamed new potatoes, and fresh fruit for dessert—passed in eager chatter about which of the spa's treatments and activities to take advantage of the next day. Only Enid was quiet and, on the surface, uninterested.

Inside, though, her emotions were seesawing. One moment she'd think that it really didn't matter if she submitted to facials and saunas and aerobics three times a day—she'd probably look exactly the same when she left Paradise Spa as she did right now. Then the next moment a wild, improbable hope would spring up in her heart. *Maybe if I go all out, if I try everything, I really will become beautiful,* she thought.

Back in their room after dinner Elizabeth changed into a nightgown and flung herself onto her bed. "So . . . do you think Chris is interested in Jessica or just being nice to her because she's a guest and it's his job?" Elizabeth asked nonchalantly.

"He probably likes her," guessed Enid. "Why wouldn't he?" She didn't add that *she'd* love to meet someone at the spa but figured it was highly unlikely that any of those glamorous guys would take notice of her.

Elizabeth patted her stomach. "The food was delicious, but I'm still hungry. I wonder if there are any vending machines around here," she joked. "I could go for a candy bar or a bag of chips!"

Enid laughed. "That would kind of defeat the purpose of the spa, don't you think?"

"The purpose of the spa . . ." Elizabeth folded her arms behind her head. "I'm not so sure about this whole 'encouraging the beautiful person within you to the surface' bit," she said. "It sounds nice, and obviously it's a good idea to have a healthy lifestyle and all that. I mean, it will feel great to be really pampered, maybe lose a pound or two. But when we go home, we'll still just be . . . us. You know? And that's OK with me."

Enid sat down on the edge of her bed to thumb through the Paradise Spa brochure. She nodded in agreement with Elizabeth, even while inside her a secret dream, an ambitious goal, was taking root and growing. She reread Tatiana Mueller's creed: "It is my firm and passionate belief that inside everyone, no matter how plain, a beautiful person waits to be discovered. . . ."

Enid couldn't admit it, even to her best friend Elizabeth. Elizabeth wouldn't understand; she'd think it was silly.

But that was because Elizabeth was *already* beautiful. Elizabeth didn't really *need* Paradise Spa. Whereas Enid . . .

I won't go back to Sweet Valley the same person as when I came, Enid vowed. *I'm going to believe in Paradise Spa and let it work its magic on me. I want to be transformed.*

Chapter 3

Jessica bounced into the dining room the next morning at the head of the Sweet Valley contingent. "I'm ravenous," she told Lila as they made their way to the buffet. "Bacon and eggs would taste great, or maybe an omelette. No, wait a minute. Pancakes and maple syrup!"

Her mouth was watering with anticipation. Then she and Lila saw what was offered for breakfast. "Plain yogurt and fresh fruit," observed Lila. "Cantaloupe, honeydew, apricots, strawberries, raspberries. And pineapple—my favorite."

Jessica wrinkled her nose at the yogurt, cruelly disappointed. "*Plain* yogurt? You mean it's unsweetened—it's not even vanilla? And where's the good stuff for putting on top, like granola?"

Lila snorted. "Granola has about a thousand

calories per spoonful. I doubt it's on the Paradise Spa shopping list!"

Dejected, Jessica filled a plate with fruit and a dollop of yogurt, then sat down with her mother and the others. "All you can drink of orange and grapefruit juice," said Elizabeth, trying to cheer her up.

"Great," said Jessica sarcastically.

Just then their waitress approached, carrying a basket covered with a white linen napkin. "We have blueberry muffins, apple-bran muffins, or whole-grain toast this morning," she announced in a soft voice. "What would you like?"

Jessica's eyes lit up. "I'll try them all!"

The waitress laughed. "How about choosing just one?" she suggested tactfully.

Jessica settled for a blueberry muffin. "I just don't see how they expect me to get enough energy eating like this," she grumbled when the waitress had moved on to the next table.

"How much energy do you need to play golf?" wondered Lila.

"More than you need sitting in a chair getting a manicure and pedicure," countered Jessica.

"You're getting a manicure?" Grace said to her daughter. "That would be fun. What do you say, Alice? After our yoga class?"

Alice nodded.

"Mom, you're doing *yoga*?" asked Elizabeth.

"Sure!" said Alice. "And I'm really looking

forward to it. Life is so busy at home, with work and my family—I hardly ever get a chance just to be quiet and contemplative. I bet a little stretching and meditation will do my mind *and* body good."

Jessica devoured her muffin and then dug into the fruit, smothering a secret smile. She was looking forward to something that would do *her* mind and body good—a couple hours of Chris the golf pro's undivided attention!

As she and Lila scanned the dining room hoping for a glimpse of Lila's mystery man, they noticed that Mrs. Mueller was making the rounds of the tables to talk to her guests. "Maybe she'll skip our table," said Lila.

"No such luck. Here she comes," hissed Jessica.

Another woman accompanied Mrs. Mueller. Like Mrs. Mueller, she was dressed in a white lab coat, but she was a bit younger, Jessica guessed—in her thirties, perhaps—and also unlike Mrs. Mueller, she was very attractive, with flawless peaches-and-cream skin, sculpted features, and silky chestnut-brown hair.

"Good morning, my dears," Mrs. Mueller chirped brightly. "I'd like you to meet my assistant, Marguerite. As you enjoy all that Paradise Spa has to offer, I hope you'll think of Marguerite—her hard work helps make it all possible."

They exchanged a few polite words with Marguerite, who then took her leave. Mrs.

Mueller, however, couldn't seem to drag herself away from her Sweet Valley visitors. She clasped her hands together, a sentimental look in her tiny eyes. "Oh, a mother-daughter retreat—how special that is!" she sang. "I cannot tell you, seeing you all so happily together . . . how it brings back delightful memories of my childhood! You see," she continued, "as a young girl I accompanied my own mother, a great Austrian beauty, to all the finest spas of Europe. That is why I was inspired to found Paradise."

Jessica exchanged a dubious glance with Lila. Hideous Mrs. Mueller's mother had been a great beauty? *That* was hard to believe.

"There's nothing, absolutely nothing, more important than the mother-daughter bond," Mrs. Mueller concluded firmly. She turned her attention to Enid. "And you, my poor little sparrow," she said in a solicitous tone, reaching out to stroke tenderly Enid's curly auburn hair. "How sad that your mother could not come. But do not worry, we will take very good care of you."

Lila kicked Jessica under the table. Lifting her napkin to her mouth, Jessica disguised a giggle as a cough.

"So." Mrs. Mueller addressed them all. "How is everything so far? Your rooms were satisfactory, no? You slept like babies?"

Everyone nodded. "The rooms are beautiful," said Mrs. Wakefield, "and I've never enjoyed a sounder, more restful sleep. There must be something about the mountain air."

"Good." Mrs. Mueller beamed. "I do want everything to be perfect for you."

"Well, actually," Jessica piped up, "my room isn't quite perfect."

Mrs. Mueller tipped her head to one side, birdlike. "No? What's the problem, my sweet?"

"We don't have a mirror," Jessica explained. "In fact, there's not a single mirror in the entire cottage. Do you think you could have one sent over?"

A dark cloud shadowed Mrs. Mueller's previously cheerful if disfigured features; her smile faded. "No," she said, her voice uncharacteristically harsh and stern. "No mirrors." She paused to draw a deep breath, and her expression softened once more. "You see," she said, patting Jessica's cheek, "there are no mirrors anywhere at Paradise Spa, not a single one, because it's *inner* beauty that matters."

Jessica shrank back from Mrs. Mueller's touch, a faint shudder moving down her spine. A pointed glance from her mother helped her decide not to pursue the issue. *Inner beauty's all that matters—baloney,* thought Jessica, disgruntled, as she spooned the last drop of yogurt from her plate. *I can definitely see why Mrs. Mueller prefers to steer clear of mirrors. But I for one like to appreciate my* outer *beauty every once in a while!*

* * *

After Mrs. Mueller left, Elizabeth pondered the woman's reaction to Jessica's question about mirrors. Retreating into her own thoughts was preferable to listening to her sister, who was now prattling on about how she couldn't wait to be alone on the golf course with gorgeous Chris. *"There are no mirrors anywhere at Paradise Spa,"* Mrs. Mueller had said, *"because it's inner beauty that matters. . . ."*

"Inner beauty—that's a strange philosophy for a place dedicated to slimming and shaping the body and perfecting skin and hair!" Elizabeth murmured to her mother.

Alice nodded. "An admirable one, though."

It must have something to do with the accident Mrs. Mueller was in, Elizabeth decided as she took a bite of fresh pineapple. Because of her appearance Mrs. Mueller was probably extra conscious that what mattered about people was how they treated others, not what they looked like. At the same time, she clearly took pleasure in surrounding herself with beauty, and with people in quest of beauty. . . .

And the people who work in the dining room are just as stunning as the rest of the staff, Elizabeth thought to herself as their waitress stopped by the table to refill coffee cups and juice glasses. The girl looked to be just a year or two older than Elizabeth, and Elizabeth gave her a friendly smile. The waitress did not smile back, however. She fulfilled her duties in a competent but somber manner, and as Elizabeth took a longer, closer look at her, she detected an infinite sadness behind the girl's large emerald-green eyes.

She ducks her head to hide her face behind her long black hair, Elizabeth observed, noting that the girl's name tag read "Katya." *Why?* The attitude of all the other Paradise Spa employees was happy and upbeat—not surprising, given the idyllic surroundings. Katya seemed to be the mysterious exception. *What's her story?* Elizabeth wondered. *Maybe she needs a friend. But how could anyone be lonely or unhappy in a wonderful, magical place like this?*

As the Sweet Valley group exited the dining room, they encountered a family of four just entering. Enid didn't remember seeing them at dinner the night before and concluded that they were brand-new arrivals.

In the friendly spirit of the spa, they stopped to make introductions. "I'm Kurt Spencer," the portly man said, "and this is my wife, Joanne, our thirteen-year-old daughter, Chelsea, and our sixteen-year-old son, Randall."

Enid saw Jessica and Lila give Randall a quick glance up and down, then stroll off without so much as a hello. *How mean,* thought Enid, stifling her anger. *Just because Randall's a little bit chubby, they decide they're not going to waste their time on him!*

Elizabeth, too, seemed to have disappeared. As Grace and Alice chatted with Mr. and Mrs. Spencer, Enid smiled at Randall. He was a nice-looking boy, despite the fact that he needed to lose a few pounds. "I think you'll like this place," Enid told him. "It's really the lap of luxury. And the food is excellent, even if there's not enough of it!"

Randall patted his waist and grinned. "That's why we're here, though," he said amiably, "to escape the temptations of a well-stocked refrigerator."

Enid laughed. "Well, good luck. I'm sure I'll be seeing you around."

"You bet," said Randall.

The Spencers moved on into the dining room, and Enid waved good-bye to Mrs. Wakefield and Mrs. Fowler, who were heading off to their yoga class. *What should I do?* wondered Enid, standing in the lobby and looking about aimlessly. There were so many options—facials and body wraps, exercise classes—and she knew she needed them all. Where to start?

She turned to look for Elizabeth and found herself face-to-face with Mrs. Mueller instead. "Oh, hi, Mrs. Mueller."

"Hello, dear. Can I help you find your way?"

"You could, except I don't know which direction I'm heading in." Enid laughed. "My skin, my hair, my muscles. Which part of me should I improve first?"

"Ah." Mrs. Mueller's eyes lit up. "May I make a suggestion? Paradise Spa offers a hair-conditioning treatment for redheads only. Like mine, my dear"—she gave Enid a maternal smile—"your hair has special needs. Will you give it a try?"

Enid nodded eagerly. "It sounds great."

Taking Enid's arm, Mrs. Mueller whisked her off down the hallway to a private salon. To Enid's surprise there was no hairstylist present; Mrs. Mueller took charge of the conditioning treatment herself.

After Enid had changed into a robe, Mrs. Mueller seated her by a sink in order to wash her hair. Then she towel-dried and combed Enid's wet hair and applied a fragrant conditioning lotion. "I will massage this into your hair for five minutes," Mrs. Mueller explained, her fingers working deftly over Enid's scalp. "It will improve the texture of your hair, mending the damage and making it silky and manageable. And it will bring out your beautiful natural highlights. You'll see—I'm sure there have been times you hated being a redhead, but now you will love it."

Enid closed her eyes, lulled into relaxation by the massage. "I do hate my hair," she confessed. "It's so frizzy—it never does what I want it to do. I'd do anything to have straight blond hair like my friend Elizabeth."

"Red hair is more striking and unusual," Mrs. Mueller said in a soothing tone. "And once we get rid of the frizzies, Elizabeth will be envying *your* hair."

Enid smiled. "That would be a nice switch!"

"You are very good friends, it is apparent," observed Mrs. Mueller, continuing to massage the conditioner through Enid's hair. "But even good friends have their moments of jealousy and competition, no?"

"It's true," Enid conceded.

"Do you envy other things about Elizabeth?"

Enid sighed heavily. "I have to admit I do. She has this fantastic relationship with her boyfriend, Todd—who, of course, is the best-looking, most popular guy at Sweet Valley High—and he just worships the ground she walks on. Whereas I . . ."

Without planning to Enid found herself pouring out the story of her devastating breakup with Hugh. Mrs. Mueller clucked her tongue sympathetically. "You poor little dove," she cooed. "And so you believe it is because you are not beautiful enough that this happened?"

"I'm sure of it," Enid said sadly.

"I will make a promise to you," declared Mrs. Mueller. "You will leave Paradise Spa with a beauty you never dreamed you could possess, and when you return to Sweet Valley, this Hugh will be on his knees begging you to take him back. And you may find you won't want to take him back, because every boy in town will be vying for your attention."

Enid smiled, caught up in the fantasy. "I like that idea. Very much!"

Mrs. Mueller was silent for a moment. Then she said, "Your friend Elizabeth . . . she has a very special relationship with her beautiful mother, Alice, does she not?"

"Oh, yes," said Enid. "Liz and Jessica are both really close to their mom. Mrs. Wakefield totally dotes on them."

"And your own mother . . ." A regretful note entered Mrs. Mueller's voice. "Why could she not come to the spa?"

"At the last minute she couldn't get away from the office. Her job's really busy right now."

"How disappointing for you."

"I was kind of hurt," Enid admitted.

"Naturally you were looking forward to being with her," surmised Mrs. Mueller. "And then she didn't have time to give you her attention when you needed it most."

"I mean, I understand," said Enid, trying to be fair. "Her job is the top priority—she's been working extra hard since she and my father got divorced. She has to."

"Ah, a divorce. When did this happen?"

"When I was in junior high." Enid's brow furrowed at the painful memory.

"And it is hardest always on the children," Mrs. Mueller remarked sympathetically.

"It's hard on everyone."

"Is it just you and your mother now? No siblings?"

"No brothers or sisters," Enid confirmed.

"But you get along."

Enid shrugged. "Most of the time. But like I said, she works pretty hard. Sometimes she gets stressed out."

"And she takes it out on you?"

"Well, I wouldn't say that exactly. But she has problems of her own, and sometimes I get the impression she just doesn't really feel like listening to mine, you know?"

Mrs. Mueller sighed. "That's very sad, because of course a mother's first duty is to be there, always, for her child. Her child *must* come first."

"I think I do come first," said Enid. "Most of the time. But like with this thing with Hugh, I've been a total wreck, and she hasn't had time to sit down and talk to me about it."

"And that probably makes you feel even worse," guessed Mrs. Mueller. "As if nobody cares about you."

Enid squeezed her eyes shut more tightly to hold back the tears. "Oh, Mom does her best," she mumbled unconvincingly.

Mrs. Mueller heaved another sympathetic sigh. Then she rinsed her hands at the sink and dried them. "There," she said brightly. "We're ready to rinse you out and put you under the dryer for a few minutes."

Enid gave Mrs. Mueller a grateful smile. Regardless of how her hair was going to look when it was all over, she felt better already. "Thanks, Mrs. Mueller," she said softly. "Thanks for listening."

Mrs. Mueller patted Enid's shoulder. "Of course, dear. Anytime."

When the Sweet Valley group dispersed after breakfast, Elizabeth looked around for Katya. She spotted the sad-looking waitress at the door to the kitchen, trading the apron she'd worn over her short skirt and T-shirt for a cotton cardigan embroidered with the Paradise Spa logo.

"Is your shift over?" Elizabeth asked in a friendly tone.

At Elizabeth's greeting Katya glanced up, startled. Then she smiled tentatively. "Yes," she replied. "Usually I go for a walk or a swim afterward, before I have to come back for the lunch shift."

"I'm Elizabeth Wakefield," said Elizabeth, extending her hand. "We just got to Paradise Spa yesterday—we're staying for a week. It seems like a wonderful place. In fact, there are so many great beauty treatments and activities, I don't know where to start!"

Katya shook Elizabeth's hand. "Many guests feel that way. But if you have a whole week, there's time to try everything at least once."

"Do the staff members get to use the facilities?" asked Elizabeth.

"Oh, yes," said Katya. "That's one of the great perks of working here."

Katya's eyes drifted to the door. "Don't let me keep you," said Elizabeth. "It's your break—you probably want some quiet time to yourself."

"Actually, no. This is fine." Katya ducked her head and smiled shyly. "It's nice to talk to you. I have plenty of time to myself. You see, I haven't been working here that long. I've made a few friends on the staff—Lulu and Terry, the other waitresses—but I still feel . . . new."

Elizabeth decided that this explained Katya's melancholy demeanor. "I'm sure it won't take much longer to feel totally at home here," predicted Elizabeth. She thought about Chris, the golf pro/chauffeur. "The other staffers I've met seem really nice."

"Oh, they are. But it's not the same as . . ." Katya's sentence trailed off, unfinished. Then she shook her head, as if to clear her thoughts. "I just had an idea, Elizabeth," she said, her tone suddenly brighter and more matter-of-fact. "Since you're new to Paradise Spa, can I spend my spare time this morning giving you and the rest of your group an insider's tour of the grounds and facilities?"

"That would be fabulous," said Elizabeth, turning to look around for Enid. "But, you know, I think everyone else has already disappeared. My mother was going to a yoga class, and my sister has a golf lesson, and I heard something else about manicures and pedicures. It looks like I'm the only one left."

"That's fine with me," said Katya, her green eyes crinkling. "Shall we?"

Elizabeth smiled. "Sure. I'd love a tour!"

They started inside, with a walk through the salons and fitness rooms. "Here are the mud baths," said Katya, opening a door. "See? You submerge yourself in one of those tubs."

Elizabeth wrinkled her nose distastefully. "Ugh. It smells like . . ."

Katya laughed at Elizabeth's expression. "Mud! Warm mud, actually. And there's peat and mineral water mixed in. It *is* odorous, but believe me, it feels great. Afterward you rinse off and then lie down for a while wrapped in warm towels. You wouldn't believe how relaxing it is, and how marvelously clean and vibrant your skin feels. You'll be tingling right down to your toes."

"I'll have to try it," said Elizabeth.

Next they peeked into the large salon where facials, manicures, and pedicures were in progress; then they visited the aerobics studio, the gym, and the steam room. "Now let's go outside," suggested Katya. "This is my favorite part of Paradise Spa."

Katya pointed out the tennis courts, the locations of various swimming pools, and the path to the golf course. "And there are countless trails for jogging and walking—the spa property extends for hundreds of acres," she said as they strolled across the grass toward a grove of flowering trees. "There's a beautiful waterfall a mile or so into the woods—when we have more time, perhaps tomorrow morning, I'll take you and your family and friends there for a swim."

Elizabeth tipped her head back, letting the bright morning sun warm her face. She took a deep breath of the air, which smelled of pine, honeysuckle, and wild grasses. "Everybody back home must think you're incredibly lucky to be working here," she remarked to Katya.

Katya lifted her shoulders. "As I said, I'm still adjusting. I'm sure soon . . ." Her voice trailed off, but she added brightly, "Everyone else on the staff thinks of the spa community as a family—most of them have been working here for quite a while, and they plan to stay forever!"

"But they're all so young," said Elizabeth. "Some of them are bound to decide on another career."

"Perhaps." Katya bent to pluck a sprig of honeysuckle. "And yes, they are young. I'm eighteen, and I'd say that's the average age—eighteen, nineteen, twenty."

"Mrs. Mueller and Marguerite are the only older people I've seen," said Elizabeth.

"It's true."

"Mrs. Mueller . . ." Suddenly Elizabeth realized she was intensely curious to learn more about the eccentric founder of Paradise Spa. "Do you like her?"

She noticed that Katya didn't answer the question directly. "Everyone on the staff thinks she's wonderful," Katya said after a moment, as if she were choosing her words carefully. "She is like a mother to them."

"And you?" Elizabeth pressed.

The sad, faraway look returned to Katya's eyes. "She's very kind, but I . . . I already have a mother." For a moment Katya was silent. Then she tossed the sprig of flowers to the ground. Turning on her heel, she walked briskly back toward the spa buildings. "Now that you've seen the whole layout, Elizabeth, you really must try one of the beauty treatments," she said, her manner artificially cheerful and brisk. "May I recommend an herbal body wrap? Mrs. Mueller guarantees it does the body *and* the soul good."

Elizabeth agreed to the suggestion, and as Katya escorted her to the salon, she resisted the urge to pry further. Katya had started to warm up to her, but when the subject had become personal—at the mention of Mrs. Mueller and Katya's own mother—she'd retreated again into her shell.

Elizabeth respected Katya's desire for privacy, but at the same time, she couldn't help wanting to know more about the beautiful, melancholy girl. With the instinct of a journalist Elizabeth was sure there was a story there. Who was Katya, and what brought her to Paradise?

"So you hold the club like this, with your left hand here and your right hand like so," said Chris, standing behind Jessica in order to demonstrate the proper grip.

Jessica was enjoying herself immensely. "Like this?" she said, purposefully sliding her hands into the wrong positions.

"No." Putting his hands on top of hers, Chris guided them into place. Then he stepped back. "There. Got it?"

"I *think* so," said Jessica, fluttering her eyelashes. "Now what?"

"Now place your feet like this and center your body right over them. Bring the club back like this. . . ." Chris demonstrated. "And swing, following all the way through."

Jessica watched him carefully and then swung her club. To her own surprise she actually hit the ball, which popped up into the air in a graceful arc.

"Hey, nice shot!" exclaimed Chris. "You're a natural."

"Really?" said Jessica. "Was that good?"

"For a beginner it was great," he assured her with a smile that made her knees knock. "So, Jessica . . ."

"Yes?" she said expectantly as they walked together to the ball she'd hit.

"Is your sister interested in golf, too?"

"My sister?" Elizabeth was absolutely the last topic Jessica wanted to discuss with Chris. "No, she's not interested in the least. In fact, she thinks it's the most boring sport ever invented."

"Oh." Chris looked a bit crestfallen. "Well, maybe she likes tennis."

"Yeah, she likes tennis," Jessica said with a touch of impatience. "So now what do I do? I want to hit it into the hole, right?"

"Right," said Chris. "That last shot was a drive, for covering long distances. Now you're going to putt—the ball will stay on the grass and roll. Back to your sister . . . you're identical twins, right?"

"Yeah, we're identical," muttered Jessica. "But we're not at *all* alike." In case Chris was getting any ideas about Elizabeth, Jessica hurried to tell him how uninteresting she was. "She's a total nerd—she actually brought her laptop computer with her to the spa! Can you believe anyone could be so geeky? Her computer and a pile of paperback books."

"She sounds very literary."

"The term is 'bookworm,'" Jessica said dryly. "She's a writer."

"A writer!" Chris's eyes lit up with interest. "Wow! I'd love to talk to her about that."

Jessica stared at him. She couldn't believe they were having this conversation. She couldn't believe Chris was actually impressed by the fact that Elizabeth spent all her spare time typing on her dumb laptop. *He's supposed to be paying attention to me!* Jessica thought, her indignation mounting. *This is my private golf lesson!*

"How's this?" Jessica called to Chris, taking a careless swipe at the golf ball.

She missed it completely; a big clump of dirt flew into the air instead. Chris didn't even notice. "I love to read and write myself," he was saying, a moony expression on his face. "That's a neat coincidence, don't you think? I'd really like to . . . that is, if you think she'd . . . Do you think she'd go out with me tonight?"

Jessica's jaw dropped. Chris was alone with *her*, privileged with the perfect opportunity to fall for *her* superior charms, and he wanted to ask out Elizabeth? *I've never been so insulted in my life!*

In response to his question Jessica whacked angrily at the little white ball, digging up another generous chunk of the golf course in the process.

"I could bring my friend Alex along—he's a groundskeeper here at the spa. We could make it a double date," Chris suggested, as if sensing he needed to placate her.

That was really too much. Jessica Wakefield wasn't anybody's charity case. "Thanks anyway," she said haughtily. "I have other plans." Dropping her club onto the grass, she brushed her hands off on her pink shorts. "I think my lesson's over. And you know what? Golf *is* the most boring sport on the planet. Liz was right about that. See ya."

Leaving her clubs for Chris to carry, she stomped off across the golf course, not even caring that she was walking right into the path of two men who were getting ready to tee off. Then she took a closer look at them. They were both young—maybe about twenty or so—and *very* cute.

Jessica flashed them a dazzling smile, and they grinned back. *Paradise Spa is crawling with gorgeous guys,* Jessica reminded herself, her spirits instantly brightening. *Who needs Chris? Liz can have him!*

Chapter 4

"I had a wonderful day," Elizabeth said with a blissful sigh as she and Enid walked to dinner. "A walk with Katya, a workout at the gym, an herbal wrap. How about you?"

"It was fun," replied Enid. "I'm exhausted, though! I took an aerobics class and I swam laps in the pool, and then I had a mud bath and a massage. Oh, and this morning Mrs. Mueller gave me a special hair-conditioning treatment designed for redheads." She touched her hair, a doubtful expression on her face. "Can you see a difference?"

Elizabeth nodded emphatically. "You look terrific," she told her friend. "I'm glad you like the spa. Tomorrow let's do some things together, OK?"

"Sure," said Enid. "Would you be up for a facial? My complexion needs major help."

"Definitely," said Elizabeth, patting her own flawless skin. "The only other time I tried one was when Jessica made me put this disgusting home-made mayonnaise-and-avocado glop all over my face—she'd read the recipe in *Teen Scene.* I was smelling that stuff for weeks."

Enid laughed. "I'm sure a Paradise Spa facial will be a more pleasant experience."

They rounded a bend in the path and nearly collided with someone hurrying in the opposite direction. When Elizabeth saw who it was, her cheeks flushed bright pink. "Chris!" she squeaked. "Hello."

"Hi, Elizabeth!" His face, too, reddened slightly; he was breathless, as if he'd been running. "You're just the person I was looking for."

Elizabeth's blush deepened. "I am?"

"I was wondering . . ." He raked a hand through his glossy dark hair, dropping his gaze shyly. "If you'd, uh . . . Your sister said you played tennis, and I thought maybe . . . you'd like to play a game or two after dinner. I mean, with me."

Elizabeth's heart skipped a beat and an eager "yes" nearly sprang to her lips. Then she remembered that Enid was standing right next to her, and she caught herself. *Enid's the one who doesn't have a boyfriend right now,* thought Elizabeth with a guilty pang. *She's the one who should be meeting people and getting asked for dates, not me.*

I won't leave her out in the cold, Elizabeth determined, her loyalty to Enid asserting itself. *She's here because of me, and I won't ditch her.* After a reassuring glance at Enid she turned back to Chris. "If you can find a fourth, we're on," she told him with a warm smile.

"No problem," said Chris with a cheerful grin. "My friend Alex would be psyched to join us—he's an excellent tennis player and a really great guy. So we'll see you two girls on the courts around eight?"

"You bet," said Elizabeth.

"Great." Chris continued to grin, clearly pleased. "So long until then."

He took a few steps backward, still smiling into Elizabeth's eyes, and then turned around and sauntered off. Elizabeth gazed after him, her heart doing one last back flip for good measure.

"You know, you didn't have to do that," Enid said irritably as soon as Chris was out of earshot.

Elizabeth blinked at her friend, snapping out of her reverie. "Hmm? What?"

"I said, you didn't have to do that," repeated Enid, her freckled cheeks hot pink with indignation. "Force Chris into dragging along a friend to make it a double date. I don't need anybody feeling sorry for me."

"I wasn't feeling sorry for you!" protested Elizabeth. "I thought playing tennis and getting to know some new people would be fun for both of us, that's all. I mean, I'd like to play tennis with

Chris, but I was also looking forward to hanging out with you tonight. But if you don't feel like it, if you're worn out after all the exercise you got today, it's really no problem. I'll just tell Chris we can't make it."

"No . . . that's OK," Enid mumbled. "Let's play tennis. You're right, it could be fun."

"And maybe Alex will be cute," said Elizabeth, dimpling mischievously. "You never know."

Enid forced a smile. "Right. You never know."

They continued on to the dining room, where they planned to meet up with Jessica, Lila, Alice, and Grace. Enid suspected that Elizabeth thought she'd overreacted to the double-date proposal, but she couldn't help feeling prickly and defensive. *Elizabeth just doesn't know what it's like to be her friend,* thought Enid, feeling more insecure about her looks than ever. *Chris walks up and suddenly I'm invisible—he only has eyes for her. It's always been like this. I'm totally in her shadow, and my only hope is that a little of the attention that comes her way will rub off on me. How pathetic.*

As they entered the dining room, Enid sneaked a peek at her reflection in the plate-glass window. What she saw didn't exactly lift her spirits. Hair that tended to frizz, skin that tended to freckle, average height, average face, average figure. *Average everything,* concluded Enid glumly. *Even Mrs. Mueller's special hair conditioner can't change that.*

They caught sight of the others, already seated at a table at the far end of the dining room. As they made their way in that direction, Enid spotted Randall Spencer, also on his way to join his family. "Hi, Randall," she said. "How was your first day at Paradise Spa?"

His cheeks were glowing from healthy exertion. "Nonstop action," he told her. "I jogged five miles, played two sets of tennis, and then hit the sauna. I bet I've lost five pounds already!"

Enid smiled. "Good for you!"

"I still have a long way to go, though," he admitted. "I'm not sure I can keep up this pace."

"Sure, you can," she encouraged him. "If you make up your mind, if you want it enough, you can do anything."

Randall nodded. "You're right. I just have to stay focused on my goals."

"I think that's the secret," she agreed.

They said good-bye and went their separate ways. Randall was basically a stranger to her, but for some reason Enid felt cheered having spoken with him. *I'm not the only person at Paradise Spa dreaming of being transformed,* thought Enid. *I'm not the only ugly duckling. I'm not alone.*

"I don't know how much more of this health food I can take," complained Jessica when their meals were served. "Or rather, how much *less.* These portions are half of what we get for dinner at home, Mom. I'm going to wither away!"

Mrs. Wakefield chuckled. "There's unlimited salad—you can fill up on that."

"Unlimited salad." Jessica rolled her eyes. "That's supposed to be a consolation?"

"I think the food is delicious," said Elizabeth, taking another bite of her lamb brochette and rice pilaf. She ate slowly, savoring every bite. "It feels good not to be stuffed, to eat just as much as you need and no more."

"Speak for yourself," said Jessica, who'd already cleaned her plate. She beckoned imperiously to the waitress. "Excuse me. Can you tell me what's for dessert? Is there ice cream tonight, by any chance?"

Everyone laughed at Jessica's hopeful tone. "I have something even better," the waitress promised.

She returned a few minutes later with a plate that held three small scoops of fruity sorbet garnished with fresh mint leaves. Jessica spooned in eagerly. "It's pretty good," she had to admit, "but I can just tell it doesn't have enough calories to really qualify as a dessert. Where's the hot-fudge sauce? Where's the whipped cream and nuts?"

"Do I hear that someone has a complaint for the kitchen?"

They all turned at the sound of the now-familiar voice. Mrs. Mueller was smiling at Jessica, who laughed. "I was just kidding around—the food is delicious," Jessica told the older woman. "I'm sure, for one week out of my life, I can survive without hamburgers and french fries!"

"Take my word for it," promised Mrs. Mueller, "with my healthy spa diet and lots of exercise, that beautiful complexion will be even more radiant and glowing a week from now. Just look at you. Such a face! And you've not yet been whisked away by the modeling agencies, the Hollywood talent scouts?" Mrs. Mueller's appreciative gaze shifted to Elizabeth. "And to think there are two of you, equally ravishing. Really, they are angels sent from heaven, are they not?"

This question was directed at Alice, who smiled as she replied, "Sometimes angels, sometimes devils."

"You should always be angels to such a charming mother," Mrs. Mueller gently lectured Jessica and Elizabeth. "And such a *beautiful* mother." She gazed with a rapt expression at Alice. "Now *this* face is perfect, exquisite. Yes, your beauty reminds me of my own mother. She had perhaps the loveliest face since Helen of Troy, a face that artists all over Europe sought to paint. Breathtaking. Unique."

Elizabeth could see that her mother was very embarrassed by Mrs. Mueller's excessive praise and fawning manner. But Mrs. Mueller seemed oblivious to her discomfort. "Yes, you girls are lucky, lucky, lucky," she prattled on, "to have mothers who dote on you and provide you with the very best opportunities life has to offer. Seeing you together, delighting in one another's company—how it reminds me of my relationship with my own dear departed mother! Ah, to return to those sweet days of youth. Cherish them, my beautiful young friends, cherish them."

Lila and Jessica were rolling their eyes at each other in a none-too-subtle fashion. Secretly, Elizabeth agreed with them—Mrs. Mueller's routine really was a bit much. *Does she gush this way to all the guests?* Elizabeth wondered. *She can't be for real. Maybe she thinks she's making us feel at home, but I wish she'd just leave us alone to enjoy the spa.*

Elizabeth looked at Enid and observed that her friend was sitting silently with slumped shoulders and downcast eyes. Obviously Mrs. Mueller's song and dance about the mother-daughter relationship made Enid feel left out, since her own mother hadn't been able to come on the trip.

Mrs. Mueller noticed Enid's dejection at the same moment that Elizabeth did. "As for you, my little lost redbird," she clucked, "will you come to me again in the morning for another beauty treatment?"

A grateful smile transformed Enid's forlorn face. "I'd like to," she told Mrs. Mueller. "Very much."

All at once Elizabeth regretted her uncharitable thoughts about Mrs. Mueller. *She's just being a good hostess,* she decided. *It's nice of her to pay special attention to Enid.*

But as much as Elizabeth wanted to, she

couldn't quite talk herself into liking Mrs. Mueller. There was something odd about the owner of Paradise Spa. . . .

"I can't shake the feeling that I've met Tatiana Mueller somewhere before," Mrs. Wakefield said to her daughters as they strolled back to Tranquillity Cottage after dinner. "Listening to her talk . . . it's not so much her face as her voice. There's something familiar about it."

"It must be all that time you spent in the spas of Europe," joked Jessica.

"That's probably it," said Alice with a laugh. "I guess I'm just imagining it."

Alone in her bedroom, however, Alice found herself still preoccupied with thinking about when she might have crossed paths with Tatiana Mueller. *It had to have been a long time ago,* she decided, *or I wouldn't have such a hard time remembering. Childhood? College? Sweet Valley back when the children were babies?*

She hadn't come up with a solution to the puzzle by the time she called her husband at home in Sweet Valley. She asked Ned about his day at the law office and then filled him in on her activities at the spa. Finally she turned the conversation to the subject uppermost in her mind. "Ned, it's driving me crazy," she told him. "I could swear I've met the woman who runs the spa, Tatiana Mueller, somewhere before. A woman about our age, reddish-gray hair, with a scar on the left side of her face. Does that name ring a bell to you? Do you think we might have known her at Sweet Valley University?"

"Tatiana Mueller . . . hmm." Alice could picture her husband's furrowed brow as he ran through his memory banks. One of the sharpest lawyers in Sweet Valley, he had a brain like a computer. "No," he said after a moment, "I can't place the name. I don't believe we knew a Tatiana Mueller in college."

"So much for that theory," said Alice with a discontented sigh. "Well, never mind, then."

They chatted for a few more minutes and then said good night. Alice replaced the telephone and sat back on her bed, a paperback novel in her hand. *Ned never forgets a name or a face,* she thought. *I'm sure he's right about Tatiana Mueller.*

She opened her book, but she couldn't concentrate on the story. As she silently read the words on the page, she seemed to hear them repeating in her head . . . and it was Tatiana Mueller speaking. Mrs. Wakefield recalled what she'd said to her daughters. *"It's not so much her face as her voice. . . ."*

The conversation with Ned hadn't helped Alice dismiss the subject of Mrs. Mueller from her mind. She had a hunch it was going to keep on bothering her. . . .

Chapter 5

"Do I look OK?" Enid asked Elizabeth as they changed into tennis togs after dinner.

Elizabeth checked out Enid's outfit, a cute combination of white shorts and a green-and-white-striped tank top. "You look adorable. Very sporty."

Enid still seemed to be insecure about her appearance. "These shorts don't make my thighs look fat?"

"Not at all," Elizabeth reassured her. "They show off your tan. Take my word for it, you look totally hot, and I'm sure Chris and Alex both will agree."

Enid laughed nervously. "I just don't want Alex to think I'm a total dog, that's all. I mean, since Chris is dragging him along on this double date when it's probably the last thing he feels like doing."

"I'm sure Chris didn't have to twist his arm too hard," said Elizabeth, grabbing her racket. "Come on, or they'll think we blew them off!"

A cool evening breeze caressed Elizabeth's skin as she and Enid walked briskly to the lighted tennis courts. As they drew closer, Elizabeth realized her pulse was racing. *Calm down,* she lectured herself. *This isn't really a* date. *Chris is just being friendly—he works here, and I'm a guest, and he probably considers it his duty to entertain me.*

But Elizabeth knew there was more to it than that. Chris had singled her out from the crowd—according to Jessica, he'd asked all sorts of questions about her. Elizabeth smiled, remembering how peeved Jessica had been when she'd learned about the tennis game. *She's had it with Chris—so much for her budding golf career!*

The two boys were waiting for them at the courts. "Elizabeth!" said Chris, his blue eyes shining. He took her hand; she felt a warm current of electricity run up her arm. "It's so nice to see you again. This is my friend Alex, who works as a groundskeeper at the spa. Alex, I'd like you to meet Elizabeth and Enid."

Like Chris and all the other Paradise Spa employees, Alex was extremely good-looking, with shaggy, sun-streaked blond hair, deep-brown eyes, and classically sculpted features. Elizabeth could see that Enid was instantly attracted to him, and he to her. *This is great!* Elizabeth thought. *Maybe Enid will find a boyfriend here, too! Wait a minute, I didn't mean it that way. I haven't found a boyfriend—I'm not looking for a boyfriend. I already have a boyfriend. . . .*

Elizabeth tried to keep in mind that Todd was waiting for her back in Sweet Valley, but when she was near Chris, she couldn't think of anything—or anyone—else. It wasn't just that he was outrageously handsome—he was also sweet, polite, witty, good-natured. . . .

The four stood around for a few minutes joking and laughing and then took sides for a doubles match. Chris and Elizabeth won the toss, so Chris served first.

His first serve was in, and Enid returned it with a forceful backhand. Elizabeth volleyed at net; Alex returned the shot with a cross-court forehand.

The furious rally continued until Enid lobbed the ball out of bounds. "I blew it," she said, crestfallen. "Sorry, Alex."

Elizabeth saw Alex pat Enid's shoulder; then he said something to her that made her laugh. Chris caught Elizabeth's eye and winked. "Fifteen love," he said in a strong, clear voice as he set up for his next serve, and Elizabeth sensed that in addition to announcing the score, he was sending her a special message. A message about love . . .

* * *

"I've just figured out the fatal flaw of Paradise Spa," declared Lila as she and Jessica drifted back toward the cottage after taking a walk after dinner. "There's absolutely no nightlife to speak of."

No nightlife . . . except on the tennis courts! Jessica thought sourly. "Did you expect it to have a disco?"

"No, but a TV in our room would be a nice touch."

"You know what Mrs. Mueller says about television."

"Yeah, yeah, yeah," grumbled Lila. She adopted a singsong falsetto. "'Paradise Spa was designed as a sylvan retreat from the cares and stresses of the cruel world, and I want my guests to bask in the peace and serenity that comes with quiet contemplation,' or some such New Age hoo-ha."

Jessica giggled. "So you're telling me after just one day you're tired of basking already?"

"I'm not tired, I'm just bored out of my—"

Lila bit off her sentence and stared into the distance. "What?" said Jessica, following her friend's gaze.

"It's him!" Lila exclaimed.

"Who?"

"Him!"

Jessica peered into the dusk. Dimly, she was able to detect the form of a tall man in a white dinner jacket. The figure was growing smaller—he was walking away from them. "What's he all dressed up for?" wondered Jessica. "Even the waiters here don't wear tuxes."

"He's *not* a waiter," declared Lila, clutching Jessica's arm. "Come on, let's catch him!"

Lila took off at a sprint, with Jessica galloping after her. "Lila, slow down!" Jessica panted breathlessly. "This isn't dignified. You don't want him to think you're some kind of desperate—"

Abruptly, Lila slammed on the brakes. Jessica ran right into her, bumping her nose on the back of Lila's head. "Ouch!" she yelped.

"Where'd he go?" demanded Lila, her hands on her hips.

Jessica rubbed her nose. "I have no idea. Don't you see him?"

"If I saw him, I wouldn't be asking you where he went," Lila snapped, crabby once more. "Shoot. I can't believe I let him get away again!"

Jessica looked from one side to the other in an effort to be helpful. Then something lying on the cobbled pathway caught her eye. "Look," she said, bending to pick it up. "A red rose."

Lila seized the rose from Jessica and held the fragrant bloom close to her face. "It was his!" she guessed with a sigh of rapture. "He was holding it and he dropped it on purpose right here—he left it as a token for me!"

Jessica raised one eyebrow. "A token? Lila, have you been reading those junky romance novels again?"

"It's from him," Lila insisted stubbornly. "I just know it."

"OK, whatever you say," said Jessica, going along with Lila's delusion. "I'm just surprised your mystery man's so shy. Why did he drop a rose and run away instead of sticking around to meet you?"

Lila took a dainty sniff of the rose. "You don't know the first thing about love, do you, Jess?" she said in a pitying tone.

Jessica shook her head. Then she noticed something: They were just fifty yards or so from the tennis courts. "Hey, let's go watch those guys play," she suggested.

"What's the point?" asked Lila. "Don't tell me you've still got the hots for Chris. I mean, not only is he the hired help, but he blew you off for your sister!"

"We don't have anything better to do," Jessica pointed out. "Come on. I just want to see what they're up to."

They found the two couples switching net sides between games. Jessica waved cheerily to Elizabeth. "Hi! What's the score?"

Elizabeth returned the wave. "Four games to two," she replied. "They're winning."

Jessica turned to look at "them" and nearly swooned. "So that's Chris's friend Alex!" she hissed, elbowing Lila in the ribs. "Check him out. Is he gorgeous or what?"

"Let me repeat two key words," Lila hissed back. "'Hired help.'"

Jessica wouldn't have cared if Alex were the Paradise Spa garbage collector. She was kicking herself for being so quick to turn up her nose at Chris's suggestion of a double date and leaving Alex to Enid, of all people. "That hair," she whispered. "That body, that smile." And he was looking straight at her!

Jessica flashed her brightest, sexiest, most inviting smile, and there was no doubt about it—Alex did a double take. Enid, meanwhile, was scowling, her usually gentle face as dark as thunder. *Get ready, gang,* Jessica thought. *The game's about to get really exciting!*

"Chris! When you introduced me to Elizabeth, you didn't tell me there was another one who looked just like her!" Alex joked as he grabbed a tennis ball and positioned himself behind the baseline. "It's a double whammy. How's a guy supposed to concentrate?"

It was Alex's turn to serve. From her place at the net Enid glanced over at the bench next to the court. Jessica had jumped on top of the bench and was pretending she was at home with the Sweet Valley High cheerleading squad. "Give me an *A* for Alex and an *A* for Ace!" Jessica shouted, kicking one of her long, slender legs high.

Enid gritted her teeth. Alex's first serve was

long. Jessica waved imaginary pom-poms. The second serve was in, and Elizabeth returned it to Alex. It was an easy shot, but he hit it into the net.

"Sorry," Alex said to Enid, his eyes glued to Jessica.

I can't believe how totally shameless that girl is, Enid thought bitterly as she stomped to the other side of the court and faced the net, her racket held high, to wait for Alex's next serve. *She'll do absolutely anything to get attention.* And the worst thing was, it worked!

Chris wasn't distracted by Jessica's antics—he was too captivated by Elizabeth to notice another girl. But Alex appeared to have forgotten he had a tennis partner. He was so busy flirting with Jessica that he hit every other shot into the net and didn't even seem to care when he and Enid quickly dropped four games in a row, losing the set.

The whole time, Jessica had been bouncing up and down on the sideline, performing her silly cheers. "Boy," Enid heard Alex say to Elizabeth as they gathered up the tennis balls and zipped the covers onto their rackets, "your sister sure has a lot of spunk!"

"Yeah," said Elizabeth with an apologetic look at Enid. "That's one way of looking at it."

As the four walked off the court to where Jessica and Lila were waiting for them, Enid was almost in tears. *We were having so much fun,* she thought. *Alex seemed to like me. Why did she have to show up and ruin everything?*

Alex strode right up to Jessica, a look of undisguised interest in his warm brown eyes. Enid dropped her gaze; she couldn't bear to watch. "So, Elizabeth, are you going to make introductions?" Alex asked.

"Alex, this is my sister, Jessica, and her friend Lila," Elizabeth obliged without enthusiasm. "Jess and Li, this is Chris's roommate, Alex—he works at the spa, too."

Alex shook Jessica's hand, holding on to it just a moment longer than was necessary. "Thanks for the pep show," he said. "Not that it helped my game."

Jessica fluttered her eyelashes. "I guess it just wasn't your night."

"Not on the tennis court, anyway," he said meaningfully.

Enid shifted her feet uncomfortably. Jessica smiled. "So, boys," she said to Alex and Chris, "I really worked up an appetite watching you run around the court. How about a trip to Paradise Station for ice cream?"

Alex and Chris exchanged a glance. "Well . . . actually, we're not supposed to leave the grounds," Chris explained.

"But you're off duty right now," said Jessica. "You go places on your days off, don't you?"

"To tell you the truth—" began Alex.

Chris interrupted him. "We have a secret stash

of ice cream in the fridge back at our room," he told the girls. "*And* we have a blender. Who's up for a milk shake?"

The idea was greeted with unanimous enthusiasm, squashing Enid's last hope that Jessica and Lila might decide they had better things to do than horn in on Enid and Elizabeth's double date.

Ten minutes later the six were making themselves comfortable in Chris and Alex's cottage and the blender was whirling. When Alex handed Enid a frothy chocolate milk shake, she gave him her brightest, prettiest smile, but the effort was wasted. He had eyes only for Jessica, and clearly the attraction was mutual.

As she watched Alex and Jessica curl up together on the love seat and start gabbing, Enid fought the urge to hurl her glass against the wall and run from the room. Elizabeth had forgotten about Enid, too; she was deep in a one-on-one conversation about writing with Chris. That left Enid and Lila . . . and neither girl was particularly thrilled to be stuck talking to the other.

"I can't believe Liz and Jess find the Paradise Spa staff so *fascinating*," drawled Lila in a tone of ultimate boredom. "I mean, at least Chris is the golf pro, but Alex! You wouldn't catch *me* throwing myself at the groundskeeper. I mean, *please*. Let's have some class!"

Enid considered Lila an unutterable snob, and ordinarily she would have sprung to the twins' defense. Under the circumstances, however, she didn't have the heart. "I guess Jessica thinks he's a nice guy," she mumbled, forcing herself to drink her milk shake even though it tasted like mud. "And he's . . . cute."

Lila snorted. "In *my* book 'cute' and 'nice' don't cut it. If you ask *me* . . ."

No one had asked Lila, but she started spouting off anyway. Enid listened because listening to Lila was preferable to watching Alex drool over Jessica. As the minutes ticked slowly and painfully by, Enid sank deeper into her chair, feeling ever smaller and more insignificant.

Thanks to the irresistible charms of Jessica Wakefield, Enid had been turned into the proverbial fifth wheel on her own double date. And she was pretty sure that at this moment, not counting the day Hugh had broken up with her, she'd never been more miserable in her entire life.

When Elizabeth saw Enid checking her watch, she told Chris that it was time to say good night. It was hard to tear herself away, though—they'd been having the most wonderful conversation. And the more time she spent gazing into his eyes, the more incredibly attractive she found him.

"Can we spend some time together tomorrow?" he asked hopefully. "How about a picnic after I finish up on the golf course?"

"That sounds great," said Elizabeth, her eyes shining. "See you then."

He touched her hand lightly as she stepped out the door. Elizabeth practically floated back to the cottage. "You wouldn't believe how much we have in common," she gushed to Enid. "We like all the same authors—he does a lot of reading in his spare time. And he writes! He keeps a journal and he even writes poetry. Don't you think that's amazing? I mean, he's so incredibly cute—that's what first drew me to him, I can't deny it—but he's also so interesting. And deep, you know? I mean, he *cares* about things. There's not a single television at the entire spa, but he reads a lot of magazines. He has really well-thought-out opinions on all kinds of issues."

As they closed their bedroom door behind them, Enid dropped onto her bed with a tired sigh. Elizabeth realized that Enid hadn't uttered a peep the whole walk home—Elizabeth had been doing all the talking. Immediately she guessed what was bothering her friend.

"I'm sorry, Enid," Elizabeth said gently, "about Jessica monopolizing Alex all night. He was really interested in you, and then she barged in and made herself the center of attention. I'm sure Alex would much rather have talked to you. She's just such a selfish brat sometimes. I don't blame you for being furious."

Enid sat up on the bed. "Actually, Liz," she said, brushing the hair back from her forehead,

"I'm not mad. I mean, there's nothing to be mad about, if you think about it. Alex had a choice between me and Jessica, and naturally he chose Jessica. Any guy would have done the same. She's much more attractive than I am—it's completely understandable."

Elizabeth blinked at Enid. "What are you talking about?" she exclaimed. "You're just as attractive as Jessica—you have different styles, that's all."

Enid shook her head, smiling sadly. "Oh, come on, Liz. We can be honest with each other about something like this. You two are classic beauties—you could be models. I'd give anything to have your looks."

Elizabeth couldn't believe her friend was talking like this. She sat down on the bed next to Enid and gave her arm a playful shake. "Enid, this is ridiculous," she lectured. "You're a really pretty girl, and you shouldn't let this thing with Alex get you down on yourself. Besides, looks aren't everything—you're a wonderful person, and that's the most important thing of all. If Alex prefers a girl like Jessica, then he deserves a girl like Jessica. If you know what I mean!"

Once again, Enid shook her head, a pensive expression on her face. "Looks *are* everything," she murmured. "Why do you think Chris fell for you? Wasn't physical attraction a big part of it?"

"Well, sure, but like I was just telling you, we have a lot more in common than—"

"No," Enid continued, without giving Elizabeth a chance to respond, "if I could take a magic pill and look like some of the girls on the staff here, I'd do it in a minute. Well, good night, Liz. I'm going to turn in."

Enid disappeared into the bathroom to wash up. Elizabeth continued to sit on the edge of the bed, Enid's words repeating in her head. "If I could take a magic pill and look like some of the girls on the staff here . . ."

Enid's right, she reflected. *It* is *as if everyone who works here took some kind of magic beauty pill.* She started to think about the unusually young and attractive employees, and the strange rule about not leaving the grounds that Chris had told her applied to all staff members, every day of the week—even when they weren't working. She pictured Katya's sad eyes and recalled the remark about her mother that hinted somehow at sorrow or loss. Suddenly Elizabeth shivered, despite the balmy air wafting through the open window. For a brief moment the enchantment of her evening with Chris faded, leaving her with a vague feeling of foreboding. Paradise Spa was a beautiful, magical place . . . wasn't it? Or was it possible that all wasn't quite as wonderful as it seemed?

Chapter 6

"Rise and shine!" Katya said cheerfully at dawn on Monday morning. "Have you all stretched out your muscles? Are you warmed up and ready to run?"

"Warmed up?" groaned Lila, doing a few half-hearted jumping jacks. "I haven't even *woken* up yet!"

Jessica yawned widely. "This *can't* be good for us," she agreed.

The Sweet Valley group and a few other spa guests, including Randall and Chelsea Spencer, had gathered outside the fitness center for a pre-breakfast run. Katya was going to show them some of the woodland trails, including one leading to a hilltop waterfall.

Katya laughed at Jessica's and Lila's complaints. "It *is* good for you," she said. "It's the loveliest time of day because you have the world all to yourself.

Besides, starting out with a brisk run gets the blood flowing. I promise you'll feel energized for the rest of the day."

Lila was still skeptical. "Money-back guarantee?"

Katya laughed again. "Well, you'd have to ask Mrs. Mueller about that!"

Elizabeth had been sitting on the lawn in a hurdle position, stretching out her hamstrings. Now she got to her feet and twisted at the waist to loosen up her back.

"OK, here we go," said Katya. "Follow me!"

Katya started out at a moderate pace—even Randall and Chelsea were able to keep up. They headed into the cool forest, dappled with golden light by the early-morning sun. Brightly colored birds chirped and trilled, glittering like jewels in the branches; with a flick of its white tail a deer bounded out of sight.

"Isn't it beautiful?" Elizabeth said to her mother. "Katya's right—this is the prettiest time of day, and I usually sleep right through it!"

"Please don't say the word 'sleep,'" Alice begged. "It's a painful reminder that if I had any sense at all, I'd still be dreaming peacefully in my bed!"

At a fork in the path Katya turned right, heading up a fairly steep slope. One by one the joggers fell back; only Elizabeth was able to stay with Katya all the way to the top of the hill. "You're in good shape," observed Katya.

Elizabeth was breathing hard; she looked with

admiration at Katya, who wasn't the least bit winded herself. "I'd love to be as fit as you," she panted. "Maybe by the end of my week at the spa, right?"

"Right," said Katya with an encouraging smile.

As they neared the crest of the hill, Elizabeth could hear the sound of running water. Suddenly, through the green tangle of trees, she glimpsed the waterfall. A stream of pure mountain water poured from the rocky peak, forming a crystal-clear pool below.

"I hope everyone wore bathing suits underneath their jogging gear like I suggested," said Katya, stripping off her T-shirt, "because this is the best place on the whole grounds to swim. The water is so cold and refreshing—it feels great after that uphill run!"

Within minutes they'd all stripped down to their suits and taken the plunge. Elizabeth gasped when she first felt how icy the water was, but after a few seconds her body adjusted to the temperature and it felt divine. "Isn't this great?" she asked her mother, who was paddling happily in the deep, clear pool.

Alice smiled rapturously. "Right now I feel about a million miles from my cluttered desk in my crazy office in Sweet Valley," she said. "I don't ever want to go back!"

Katya stroked across the pool in their direction.

"What kind of work do you do?" she asked Mrs. Wakefield.

"I'm an interior designer," Alice replied. "I have a partner named Doug—it's a small firm. But business was so good last year, I'm starting to think we may be ready to take on a third partner. It's nice to be busy, but I don't like having to work late every night—it cuts into my time with my family."

"Your family comes first, then," said Katya.

Mrs. Wakefield smiled at Elizabeth. "It sure does."

As Katya and Alice chattered on about different subjects, Elizabeth realized it was the first time she'd seen her new friend this animated. *She really likes Mom,* Elizabeth concluded. Then she remembered the faraway look in Katya's eyes when she'd mentioned her own mother during their conversation the previous day. She also recalled the rule about employees not leaving the grounds. Did that mean they could go home only when they had their annual vacation? *Maybe that's why Katya seems so sad at times,* Elizabeth guessed. *Maybe her family doesn't live nearby—they could even live in another state—so she doesn't get to see them that often. She's homesick!*

After swimming the group sat for a while on a large, flat sun-warmed rock to dry off, then headed back down the hill at a walk. Elizabeth fell into step beside Katya. "Your mother is a very special person," Katya said to Elizabeth. "You are lucky, the three of you, to be together like this."

Elizabeth nodded in wholehearted agreement. "What about you?" she asked. "Has your mother visited you at the spa since you started working here?"

To Elizabeth's surprise something like fear flickered across Katya's face. When she spoke, her voice was rough with dread as well as sorrow. "No—no, because . . . I ran away from home, and I can't ever go back," she burst out. "I—I—" After an agonizing pause Katya choked out the shocking words. "I'll never see my mother again!"

Despite Katya's efforts at self-control, a sob escaped her. Her eyes flooding with tears, she turned quickly away from Elizabeth. "Katya, are you all right?" Elizabeth asked, her heart brimming with sympathy and concern. She reached out to touch the other girl's arm. "Can I help you in any way? Do you want to talk about it?"

Katya didn't reply. Whirling away from Elizabeth's hand, she raced down the path into the densely tangled undergrowth and disappeared from sight.

Enid, who'd been chatting with Randall Spencer, caught up to Elizabeth at the bottom of the hill. "Where's our fearless leader?" she asked.

Elizabeth's forehead furrowed. "She went on ahead," she answered. "To tell you the truth, without intending to I said something to upset her. I asked about her family, and she told me she ran away from home. Then she burst into tears and hurried off."

"A runaway—the poor thing!"

"It's terrible, and I'm worried about her," Elizabeth agreed. "I mean, at least she has a good job, and Mrs. Mueller seems to take a real interest in her employees. But she's clearly so unhappy."

They'd reached the main spa buildings, and Elizabeth pushed open the glass door to the lobby, hoping to locate Katya. Katya was nowhere in sight; Mrs. Mueller, however, was just emerging from her office, and with a cheerful wave she headed in their direction.

"Such early birds!" she exclaimed. "And look at you, glowing with health. But what's this!" She peered closely at Enid's face. "You've been sitting in the sun—tsk tsk!"

Enid hung her head guiltily. "I know I shouldn't, since I have sensitive skin. But it was just for a few minutes, and it felt so good. . . ."

Mrs. Mueller chuckled. "Fortunately, you are still young—there is time for you to learn to take care of your skin properly before permanent damage is done. In the meantime Paradise Spa can help you with your little freckle problem. I'll make an appointment for you with Wilhelmina, our skin-care consultant. Let's see . . . you and I have a session at two. How about one o'clock with Wilhelmina in Salon Number Four? Good, good."

Mrs. Mueller bustled off to talk to some of her

other guests. Elizabeth, who'd been stifling a giggle, burst out laughing the instant Mrs. Mueller was out of earshot. "Ah, yes, Miss Rollins," she joked, "and how long have you been suffering from this little freckle problem?"

Enid didn't join in Elizabeth's laughter. "Do you really think they can do something about my freckles?" she asked hopefully, putting a hand to her face. "Oh, what I wouldn't do to have a peaches-and-cream complexion like yours!"

"But, Enid, there's nothing wrong with a few freckles," Elizabeth pointed out. "They match the rest of you. I mean, your hair, your eyes . . . you'd look *naked* without them."

"Maybe I'll change my hair, too," said Enid. "Mrs. Mueller's special conditioning treatments are improving the texture—she says she can get rid of the frizz altogether."

"Enid." Elizabeth looked her friend straight in the face. "You're not really thinking of keeping this appointment with Wilhelmina, are you?"

"Of course I am!" declared Enid, her eyes glowing with the zeal of a convert. "I wouldn't miss it for the world. Oh, Liz, isn't Paradise Spa wonderful?"

"This is disgusting," whined Lila as she eased herself gingerly into the warm, gloppy mud bath. "This is absolutely foul. Ugh—and that *stink*!"

Submerged to her neck in mud in the single-person tub next to Lila's, Jessica had been holding her breath. Finally, though, she needed to get some air into her lungs. With a gasp she inhaled deeply, getting a good, strong whiff of mud. She nearly gagged. "It smells like a swamp. And we have to sit in it for how long?"

The attendant laughed. "Just ten minutes."

"It'll feel like the longest ten minutes of my life," Lila predicted gloomily.

"Oh, I don't know," said Jessica, wiggling her fingers and toes. She was starting to get used to the smell, and she decided the mud wasn't so bad. "Just think about all the impurities that are being sucked out of our pores. And it's so nice and warm—relaxing, don't you think?"

"It weighs a ton," Lila complained. "I feel like I've been buried alive."

"Try to have a positive attitude," Jessica counseled. "Think of how unbelievably beautified we're becoming. Think of how envious everyone at Sweet Valley High is going to be when we get back to school and—"

"Ooh!" Lila squealed, nearly leaping out of her mud bath.

"Are you OK?" shrieked Jessica, thinking that maybe the temperature of Lila's mud had been accidentally turned up and she was being boiled alive.

Lila's voice dropped to a loud whisper. "It's him!" When she lifted her arm to point, gobs of mud flew in every direction—one hit Jessica square in the face.

"Geez, Li, would you . . . !" Jessica sputtered. She wiped her face, but since her hands were muddy, too, that only made matters worse. The attendant tried dabbing at her eyes with a towel; Jessica squinted after Lila's mystery man.

Sure enough, it was him. Wearing a terry-cloth robe and sandals, he was visible beyond the tinted glass that walled the salon, strolling down the hall. "Do you think he's going to take a mud bath?" Lila asked, glancing in panic at the unoccupied tub next to her. "Ohmigod, what if he does? What will I do? I'm *naked* under all this mud!"

Her concern was for nothing; the mystery man had disappeared. "These are the women's tubs," Jessica reminded Lila. "Men's are separate, remember?"

"That's right." Lila wilted back into the mud. Then she sat up straight again, jack-in-the-box style. "Is my time up yet?" she asked the attendant. "Can I get out now?"

Five minutes later the two girls were thoroughly rinsed and dried. "Now for the fun part," said Jessica. "They wrap us in steaming towels, and we get to take a little nap in one of those dark rooms. Doesn't that sound great?"

Lila had something else in mind. "Come on," she said, tightening the belt on her robe and seizing Jessica by the arm.

"Where are we going?"

"The men's spa," Lila hissed.

Jessica's eyes widened. "Lila, we can't! They're . . . they're not wearing any clothes in there!"

Lila grinned. "So? The cheerleaders peeked in the boys' locker room at SVH once, didn't they?"

"I never—" Jessica began indignantly.

"Oh, please. Don't be such a prude."

With Lila in the lead they slipped unnoticed from the women's half of the spa. Jessica balked just shy of the door to the men's half. "This is as far as I go," she whispered to Lila. "You're nuts, you know that?"

"You're a wimp, you know that?" Lila retorted.

The male attendant had his back turned; Lila tiptoed past him. Jessica hid behind a pillar, ticking off the seconds in her head. *One thousand one, one thousand two—boy, are you going to get us in trouble, Li!—one thousand three, one thousand four . . .*

Suddenly Lila sprinted back into view, her robe flapping. She collapsed against Jessica, giggling hysterically. "Let's get out of here," she hiccuped.

Safe in the women's shower room, Jessica pumped Lila for details. "So did you see him? Did you see *all* of him?"

Lila shook her head. "He wasn't there," she said regretfully. "The only people I saw were"—she clutched at Jessica, the laughter bubbling up again—"pudgy Randall Spencer and his even pudgier dad!"

Jessica burst out laughing, too. "Eew!" both girls squealed in unison.

Chris was waiting for Elizabeth near the golf course with a big wicker picnic basket. "I wish I could tell you that there was a hunk of cheese and a chocolate cake in here," he said in greeting, "but it's spa fare. Light and healthy."

Elizabeth laughed. "That's fine with me. I'm getting used to it, actually, and I feel great. I should try to stick with it when I get back home—maybe I'll give up junk food altogether." Then she shook her head, smiling. "Naw."

They strolled off together across the grass. "I'm going to take you to my favorite place at Paradise Spa," Chris told her. "It's a bit of a walk, though—hope you don't mind."

"Is it the waterfall?" asked Elizabeth.

"Close," said Chris. "You'll see!"

A short hike took them to the top of a small hill not far from the waterfall where Elizabeth, Katya, and the others had gone swimming that morning. About a hundred yards down the other side, Chris led Elizabeth over to the bank of a burbling stream. Trees grew close to the stream, their dense green foliage nearly blocking out the sun, and wild flowering shrubs scented the damp air with an exotic perfume. "See?" said Chris, pointing.

Elizabeth found herself gazing into the mouth of a small moss-covered cave. The entrance was laced with blossoms and greenery; just inside, a flat rock made a perfect natural picnic table. She let out a gasp of surprise and pleasure. "This is beautiful!" she exclaimed.

"Isn't it?" said Chris. "I stumbled on it a few months back. Now I finally have someone to share it with." He extended an arm in a sweeping, mock-gallant gesture. "After you, madam."

Ducking her head, Elizabeth stepped under the flowers and vines into the cave. Chris spread a checkered cloth onto the rock and opened the picnic basket. "We have raw vegetables and fresh fruit—of course," he said. "Also sandwiches: sliced turkey, low-fat cheese, and sprouts on whole-wheat pita bread."

He poured two cups of herbal iced tea from a thermos, and they dug into the lunch. As Elizabeth studied his face, it occurred to her that despite the intimacy of the setting, he was still nearly a stranger to her. And she wanted to know everything about him. "I didn't get around to asking you last night," she began. "How old are you?"

"Eighteen," replied Chris. He cocked an eyebrow at her, smiling. "An older man. Is that OK?"

"Sure," said Elizabeth, blushing slightly. "If you don't mind a younger woman."

Lifting an arm, he brushed her face lightly with his fingertips. "You don't seem young," he said. "I mean, you seem older than your sister, even though I know you're the exact same age. Older in a good way."

"Sometimes I feel like Jessica's mother instead of her sister," she admitted, laughing. "So." She took a carrot stick from the basket of crudités. "Are you thinking of making a career out of working at health spas, or being a golf pro somewhere?"

"Maybe," said Chris after a moment's consideration. "I don't really know. When I decided to put off college for a while, this seemed like a fun interim job. I'm pretty happy here—I could see staying for a while."

"I'm glad you're happy," said Elizabeth, her eyes shadowing, "because I've been talking to Katya. You know, the new waitress? And I get the feeling . . ." It struck her that Chris might be a source of information about the mysterious Katya. "Do you know her, by the way?"

"Just to say hello to. She hasn't been here very long—doesn't socialize much with the other staffers. I get the impression she's shy."

"Maybe a little." *Shy, but mostly terribly lonely and sad,* Elizabeth mused, deciding to keep mum about Katya's past—it looked as if she hadn't shared the tale with her co-workers. *She ran away from home—why? And why doesn't she feel she can ever go back?*

Chris wouldn't be able to help her find answers to these questions, so Elizabeth put them out of her mind. It wasn't too difficult. When she was with Chris, she found it hard to think of anything but him. Sweet Valley . . . and Todd . . . seemed light-years away. . . .

They finished their lunch, chatting idly about Alex and Jessica, and some of the celebrity guests Chris had given golf lessons to. When they were done, Chris packed up the hamper. Then for a moment they sat in silence, listening to the music of the birds and the nearby brook. Elizabeth was first to break the spell. "This is a magical spot," she said softly. "Like something from a fairy tale, or Shakespeare's *Midsummer Night's Dream*."

Chris touched her hand. "The most magical thing about it is that you're here with me."

Suddenly he was pulling her close to him, and Elizabeth didn't resist. Caressed by birdsong in the dappled green light of the cave, it seemed the most natural thing in the world to wrap her arms around Chris's waist and lift her face to his for a kiss. And when his lips met hers, Elizabeth could feel it from the top of her head to the tips of her toes. Magic.

Chapter 7

Enid's face was still stinging from her freckle-fading treatment with Wilhelmina when she knocked on the door of Mrs. Mueller's office. *I guess that's how I know the cream is working,* she thought to herself. *No pain, no gain!*

"Come in, come in," Mrs. Mueller called.

The spa's director was seated behind a large desk flanked by tall bookshelves, busily scribbling in a notebook. Enid entered the office, a shy smile on her face. "Sorry to intrude," she said. "I wasn't sure if I was supposed to meet you here or at the salon where we met yesterday."

Mrs. Mueller closed the notebook and beamed at Enid. "Sit, sit," she invited warmly. "This chair right here. Let's just talk for a few minutes before the hair treatment, shall we?"

Enid relaxed in the plush easy chair next to

Mrs. Mueller's desk. "So how are you today?" Mrs. Mueller asked, leaning forward in a way that made Enid feel she really cared about the answer.

"Oh, I'm OK." Enid shrugged. "My appointment with Wilhelmina went fine. I guess," she added doubtfully. "Can you see a difference?"

"Oh, certainly," said Mrs. Mueller. "And your friends, your beautiful friends? Elizabeth, Jessica, and Lila. Are they enjoying the spa?"

"I'll say." Enid couldn't prevent a note of bitterness from stealing into her voice. "Elizabeth is off on a picnic with Chris, the golf pro. And Jessica is probably cuddling up someplace with Chris's friend Alex. It's just not fair!" The words burst out almost against Enid's will. "Alex was supposed to be my date, and then Jessica came along and . . . It's just not fair," she repeated glumly.

Mrs. Mueller clucked her tongue. "My poor little sparrow. Yes, it's true, it does seem that all good things come to girls like Elizabeth and Jessica, the blond-haired, blue-eyed beauties of the world. It isn't fair to the little sparrows, no, it isn't fair at all."

"Liz is my best friend—I don't like to be jealous of her," said Enid, shifting uncomfortably in the chair. "I hate myself when I feel this way, but sometimes—especially lately—I can't help it. I just get in this *mood.*"

"Well, let's see if we can help you to a more tranquil place," suggested Mrs. Mueller, her melodic voice growing low and velvety. "Close your eyes, Enid, and think about things that bring you pleasure and serenity. Think about the lapping of ocean waves against the shore, and an armful of fresh, fragrant flowers, and a starry night with a round, opalescent full moon, and a young mother crooning a soft lullaby to her newborn babe . . ."

Obediently, Enid closed her eyes. Mrs. Mueller's voice wrapped tenderly around her, and she listened, allowing herself to be lulled half to sleep. And then it was as if the voice were inside her own head—as if it came from her own consciousness.

"Enid, can you hear me?"

Enid felt herself floating outside of her body. Her eyes were still closed, but her mind was full of colors and sounds and sensations: the sea, the flowers, the moon, the lullaby. She nodded. "Yes."

"Are you here with me at Paradise Spa?"

"Yes."

"But now you are going back to Sweet Valley. You are going home."

Enid felt herself floating . . . and sure enough, she was in the front yard of her house in Sweet Valley, in the kitchen, in her bedroom. "Yes, I'm home now," she responded.

"And your mother has just arrived home from work. She is in a bad mood, and she picks a fight with you about chores around the house."

Enid frowned. Could she really hear her

mother's voice, raised in anger? "I don't remember her ever yelling at me about—"

"She is yelling now. She says she is fed up with you. She says she wishes you lived with your father instead of with her. She says that if it weren't for you, perhaps her marriage to your father wouldn't have fallen apart."

Enid swallowed; her throat was salty with tears. "Does she really feel that way? She never told me that. How can she blame me for what happened between her and Dad? I've always tried so hard to be helpful. . . ."

"You *have* tried hard," said Mrs. Mueller soothingly. "You've done everything possible to make your mother's life easier, to make your life together work. But she doesn't appreciate your efforts."

"If only she'd talk to me about it," Enid said plaintively. "If only she'd tell me what I'm doing wrong."

"She's a somewhat selfish woman," said Mrs. Mueller. "Perhaps she never really wanted to have a child. She feels she has enough problems of her own without having to worry about *your* problems and needs."

"But I love her." Enid felt a tear slide down her cheek. "Doesn't she love me?"

"Not all mothers love their offspring," Mrs. Mueller said sorrowfully. "Not all mothers put their children first, make their children feel good about themselves. Now, Enid. Are you listening carefully to me?"

"Yes."

"You are returning to Paradise Spa. You are seated again in my office."

"Yes."

"And while the substance of this conversation will remain in your mind, you will not remember that you were in a hypnotic state."

"Yes."

"Enid, come back to me. Enid, wake up."

Enid blinked her eyes. The light in Mrs. Mueller's office seemed unnaturally bright. "I'm sorry," she murmured. "I drifted off there for a moment."

"It's all right," Mrs. Mueller assured her. "Now, where were we?"

"We were talking about how beautiful Elizabeth is, and how plain I am," said Enid woefully.

Mrs. Mueller smiled. "You are *not* plain," she said firmly. "In fact, I believe you have the potential to be a very beautiful young woman yourself."

A ray of hope illuminated Enid's glum expression. "You do?"

"I do, indeed. It is my business, is it not? Discovering the beauty in each individual and bringing it forth into the sunshine?"

Enid nodded eagerly. "Can you do that for me?"

"I can," Mrs. Mueller confirmed, "if you are willing to devote yourself wholeheartedly to the diet, exercise, and beauty regimen I prescribe for you, a regimen that I will design exclusively for you."

"I'll do whatever you say."

Mrs. Mueller smiled. "Good. There will be vitamin supplements in addition to your spa meals, and we'll continue the skin and hair treatments. Can you be faithful?"

"Yes. Yes!" Enid burst out laughing. Suddenly she felt as light and carefree as a seagull cavorting on an ocean breeze. *Mrs. Mueller cares about me—she's going to help me!* she thought ecstatically. "I'll try anything if it means I'll leave Paradise Spa looking and feeling like a new person!"

"Oh, you'll feel like a new person, my dear," Mrs. Mueller promised. "You will."

"Elizabeth," a sweet voice called out behind her. "Elizabeth, may I speak with you?"

Elizabeth, who was just about to sit down in a lounge chair next to one of the mineral pools, turned to see Katya waving to her. She waved back, and Katya hurried to join her. "I just wanted to . . . apologize," Katya said, ducking her head, "for running off like that this morning. It's a painful subject and sometimes I can't bear to . . . You understand."

Elizabeth's heart went out to the girl. "Of course I do," she said gently.

"I didn't mean to offend you," said Katya.

"You didn't, don't worry," Elizabeth assured her. "And I didn't mean to pry."

Katya smiled, relieved. "So we're still friends?"

Elizabeth smiled back. "Of course!"

"Good." Katya clapped her hands together, pleased. "Because I have the afternoon off, and I thought perhaps we could do something fun together, you and me and some of the other younger guests. How about a game of golf?"

Elizabeth wrinkled her nose. On the one hand, she was falling hard and fast for the Paradise Spa golf pro, but on the other . . . "It's not really my sport. I don't even know how to play," she said without much enthusiasm.

Katya's eyes danced mischievously. "Actually, I was thinking about Frisbee golf. What do you say?"

Elizabeth laughed. "In that case . . . sure!"

It was a lively group that gathered in the forest behind the spa later that afternoon. Each armed with a Frisbee, Elizabeth, Jessica, Lila, Katya, Chris, Alex, and Randall—everyone but Enid, whom Elizabeth figured must be having one of her special antifreckle treatments—took turns aiming for the targets Katya had staked out in the woods.

"This seventh hole is really a killer," said Chris, flicking his Frisbee in the direction of the dead tree stump projecting from an outcropping of rock over a creek.

He'd been shooting for an opening between two tree trunks, but he misfired and the Frisbee hit one of the trees, ricocheting back at him. Jessica, meanwhile, had flung her Frisbee haphazardly, and now it was stuck in a tangle of ivy. Alex lifted her up on his shoulders to retrieve it, but they were both laughing so hard, it was all they could do to remain upright.

Katya and Elizabeth were vying for the lead, running and laughing through the trees. Katya's Frisbee hit the stump first. "Bingo!" she shouted triumphantly.

Elizabeth paused to get her breath, bending over with her hands on her knees. Suddenly someone grabbed her from behind, and she gasped.

"Ssh." Swiftly, Chris pulled her behind the thick trunk of an old, gnarled tree. Folding her in his arms, he gave her a long, deep kiss. *So much for catching my breath!* Elizabeth thought, her heart pounding faster than ever.

"Having a good time?" asked Chris, kissing her again.

"Oh, yes," murmured Elizabeth, her eyes starry. "I never thought I'd enjoy golf quite this much!"

Hand in hand and grinning ear to ear, they rejoined the others. Katya was pointing deeper into the woods. "I think the eighth hole is that way," she called. "It's a big boulder with another boulder balanced on top of it. Ready, set, go!"

Seven Frisbees flew through the woods, and a second later seven teenagers galloped after them. Randall was ahead for a moment, but then he tripped on a tree root. Playfully elbowing Alex out of the way, Jessica reached her Frisbee first. She picked it up and lobbed it with all her might over a dense thicket.

Elizabeth was right on her sister's heels. Plunging through the thicket, they suddenly found themselves standing at the verge of an open meadow. "Look. What do you suppose that is?" said Jessica, pointing across the field.

Elizabeth stared at the large windowless building, glowing bright white in the afternoon sun. "I have no idea. Let's ask—"

She turned to look for Katya and was just in time to see Katya, Chris, and Alex emerge from the thicket. The three spa employees stopped dead in their tracks, their eyes wide with shock.

"Oh, I—I didn't mean to lead us in this d-direction," Katya stuttered, the color draining from her face. "Come on, everyone, back the way we came. This is private property—we're not supposed to be here. *Hurry!*"

A desperate note had entered Katya's voice. Quickly, Elizabeth, Jessica, Lila, and Randall gathered up their Frisbees and trotted back into the cover of the forest.

"I think the game is over," Katya said, glancing over her shoulder in a fearful fashion. "Jessica, you won. And now I really need to get back to the spa. . . ."

Striding briskly, Katya led the group through the woods, away from the forbidden meadow. Elizabeth could hear her sister and Lila whispering, speculating about the mysterious white building. Elizabeth, too, was curious. She glanced inquiringly at Chris, but he just shook his head without speaking. And Katya was so visibly shaken, Elizabeth didn't want to upset her further by asking any of the questions that were crowding into her mind.

What was the windowless building? Was it part of Paradise Spa? If so, why was it private and hidden away in the woods, and why were Katya, Alex, and Chris scared to death because they'd accidentally disclosed its presence to some of the guests?

"I'm going to be sore tomorrow," Elizabeth said to Enid as they stretched out on the floor after a vigorous aerobics class later that afternoon.

"Tell me about it," groaned Enid. "What a workout. I was using muscles I didn't even know I had!"

Slowly, they rose to their feet. Patting their damp faces with towels, they left the aerobics studio, heading back through the main spa building. "A shower will sure feel good," anticipated Elizabeth. "And then maybe a nap before dinner."

Enid laughed. "I may sleep right through dinner until breakfast tomorrow!"

Elizabeth shook her head. "Not me. After all the calories I burned today, if I missed a meal, I'd probably keel over."

"I guess I didn't get quite as much exercise as you. What did you say you did—played Frisbee golf? That must have been when I was meeting with Mrs. Mueller."

"So how did all your special appointments go?" asked Elizabeth.

"Really well," Enid replied. "Mrs. Mueller is so supportive and encouraging. She really takes a personal interest in her clients, you know?"

"She seems to like you a lot, that's for sure," commented Elizabeth. "And what did you think of Wilhelmina?"

"She's a miracle worker," said Enid. Elizabeth thought she was joking, but Enid's expression was earnest. "Look at my complexion, Liz. Can't you see an improvement?"

Elizabeth studied Enid's face. The skin was faintly pink, as if it had been irritated. "Your freckles have definitely faded a little, but like I said before, I've always thought you have a beautiful complexion, so in my humble opinion, getting rid of your freckles isn't necessarily an 'improvement.'"

"Well, *I* think it is," declared Enid with a toss of her hair. "And if you'd been stuck with freckles all your life, I'm sure you'd agree."

Elizabeth didn't want to pick a fight. "Maybe," she said with an amiable shrug.

After walking past a few more fitness studios, they rounded a corner. On their left were offices, including Mrs. Mueller's. As they approached, they heard a voice raised in anger; someone was receiving a fierce lecture.

Elizabeth glanced in surprise at Enid. She recognized the voice—it belonged to the usually benevolent and sweet-tempered Mrs. Mueller!

Snatches of the conversation drifted into the corridor through a half-open door. "I told you never to . . . how dare you defy . . . you know what will happen if you transgress . . . if you ever . . ."

The voice dropped; now Mrs. Mueller's words were inaudible, but if anything, her tone was even more threatening. They could hear someone crying. Then, suddenly, Katya burst from the office, her hands covering her face. The door slammed behind her.

Elizabeth started toward Katya, but the girl hadn't seen her. Still sobbing, Katya darted down the hall and disappeared.

Elizabeth and Enid stared after her. "Boy, that was really strange," said Elizabeth. "Poor Katya. I wonder what she did—" Elizabeth's eyes flashed with intuition. "Wait a minute. I wonder if this has something to do with the white building."

"What white building?" asked Enid.

Elizabeth described the incident in the woods during the Frisbee golf game, and Katya's distressed reaction. "She said the building was private. Somehow Mrs. Mueller must have found out about it. But I can't believe she'd come down so hard on Katya over something that was clearly an innocent mistake."

"I'm sure Mrs. Mueller has Katya's own well-being in mind," declared Enid, jumping unexpectedly to Mrs. Mueller's defense. "If Katya broke an important rule of the spa, she deserves a reprimand."

"But you saw Katya—she was crying her eyes out!" said Elizabeth, astonished by Enid's insensitivity.

"If you ask me, Katya's oversensitive," responded Enid. "I'm sure Mrs. Mueller was being completely fair with her. She seems to have a very good relationship with all her employees—if Katya's not getting along at the spa, I'm sure it's her own fault."

Elizabeth didn't know how to reply; she was flabbergasted. Almost more puzzling and disturbing than the scene between Katya and Mrs. Mueller was Enid's reaction.

Enid's complexion wasn't the only thing about her that seemed to be changing. *What's happening to my friend?* wondered Elizabeth.

Elizabeth shouted good-bye to Enid, who was still in the bathroom getting ready for dinner. "I have an errand to do—I'll meet you at the dining room, OK?"

"Fine. See you there," Enid called back.

Elizabeth hurried along the path to the dining room. She found the kitchen staff busy setting tables, and as she'd hoped, she spotted Katya, moving from table to table with a tray of water goblets.

"Katya, I'm glad I found you," said Elizabeth, stepping to the other girl's side.

When Katya heard Elizabeth's voice, she nearly dropped a goblet. "Oh. Elizabeth. Hello," she said, her voice low and strained.

"Katya, about this afternoon and the white building," Elizabeth began. "I hope we didn't get you into trouble with Mrs. Mueller."

At the mention of the white building Katya's eyes grew wide; her hand started to shake as she placed the goblets on the table. *She's scared,* Elizabeth realized. *She's scared to death!*

"Oh, it's not a problem," Katya mumbled. "We should do something fun together again soon. You play tennis, don't you? Perhaps we could organize a round-robin competition. Now, you must excuse me. Dinner starts in just a few minutes and I still have much to do. . . ."

Grabbing her empty tray, Katya hurried back to the kitchen. Elizabeth stared after her. *She was pretty eager to change the subject,* she noted. *She doesn't want to talk about the white building . . . or maybe she's not supposed to. What's going on?*

"So there Grace and I were in the yoga class," Alice was telling the others at dinner, "and of course, even though it's only the second day I've done yoga, I feel like I'm ready to try some of the more advanced positions. *Well.*" She smiled ruefully. "There are just some things the human body isn't meant to do. I managed to twist myself into the Serene Swan position . . . but then I got stuck!"

"She was like a pretzel," Mrs. Fowler confirmed. "Luckily I was there to unbend her."

The girls burst out laughing. "Mom, you're a nut," Elizabeth said with affection.

"You'd better take it easy," Jessica teased. "Dad will never forgive us if we don't bring you home in one piece."

Lila shook a finger at her own mother. "That goes for you, too, Mom," she lectured with mock sternness. "I don't want to hear about your doing the Serene Swan routine. Geez—who'd have thought you could get into so much trouble in a *yoga* class!"

Elizabeth and Enid got up to go to the buffet and refill their soup bowls with gazpacho. The cold tomato-based soup was spicy and refreshing . . . and very low-fat, so they were allowed to eat as much of it as they liked.

"This is my favorite time of day here," Elizabeth said to Enid as she ladled gazpacho into her bowl. "It's so much fun to talk about all the wacky spa things we've all been experimenting with. I can't remember when I felt this close to my mother." Elizabeth's eyes strayed to the kitchen; she couldn't help thinking about poor Katya, the runaway. "I'm so lucky to have such a great mom," she added. "I can't imagine my life without her."

Enid bit her lip. "I wish I could say the same," she muttered.

Elizabeth cocked her head. "What do you mean? Your mom is terrific!"

"I don't know about that," said Enid. "She doesn't do any of the things a mother's supposed to do for a daughter—support and encourage her, boost her self-esteem."

"Enid, that's just not true!" exclaimed Elizabeth. "You two have a great relationship."

"Maybe we just put up a good front," said Enid. Ladling some gazpacho into her bowl, she turned to head back to the table. "Appearances can be deceiving."

Elizabeth trailed after Enid, baffled by her negative outburst. *What's been eating Enid? Maybe her feelings are still hurt because her mother couldn't come to the spa,* Elizabeth speculated. *I can understand why she'd be a* little *mad. Still—to say something that extreme, that hostile . . .*

Tonight the Sweet Valley group was being waited upon by a beautiful tawny-haired girl named Sierra; Katya was taking care of a few tables on the other side of the dining room. Whenever she walked back to the kitchen, however, Katya glanced in their direction. And even from a distance Elizabeth could see the longing in her emerald-green eyes.

It's Mom, Elizabeth thought. *Katya really likes her. And seeing us all together when she misses her own mom so much . . .*

"I really feel sorry for Katya," Elizabeth said to Alice. "She told me today that she ran away from home, and for some reason she feels like she can't go back. And I get the impression that she's not really happy working here." She didn't mention the conversation she'd overheard between Katya and Mrs. Mueller. "The worst thing is, she says she hasn't even talked to her mother since she started working at Paradise Spa, but I can tell she really misses her."

"That's terrible!" exclaimed Mrs. Wakefield. "The poor thing. And I can imagine how her mother feels—if you or Jessica ever . . . !" She shook her head sadly. "The poor woman must be worried absolutely sick."

Suddenly Elizabeth had an idea. "Mom, what if *you* talked to Katya?" she suggested. "She's really private, and she clammed up with me, but I bet she'd open up to you. You might be able to talk her into getting in touch with her mother, and maybe even returning home!"

"It's worth a shot," agreed Alice. "I'll see if I can find some time alone with her."

Elizabeth felt better about Katya already. "Thanks, Mom," she said, squeezing her mother's hand. "You're the greatest, did you know that?"

Mrs. Wakefield smiled. "Thanks, kiddo. I think you're pretty special, too."

As she gazed at her mother, Elizabeth had an odd sensation that someone was watching them. She turned slightly, expecting to see Katya looking their way. Instead she noticed Mrs. Mueller standing in the entrance to the dining room staring at their table. *Staring at us,* Elizabeth thought. *No . . . she's staring at Mom.*

It was true; Mrs. Mueller's strangely intense gaze was fixed on Alice Wakefield's face. And her expression . . . it reminded Elizabeth of the tone she'd heard Mrs. Mueller use with Katya that afternoon. There was something surprisingly fierce in her eyes, something almost . . . cruel.

When Mrs. Mueller realized Elizabeth was gazing back at her, she smiled in acknowledgment and then turned away. A chill ran down Elizabeth's spine; she wasn't quite sure why.

"Mom, didn't you say you thought you'd met Mrs. Mueller before?" Elizabeth asked. "Did you ever figure out where?"

Mrs. Wakefield shook her head. "It never came to me. I should just ask Tatiana—maybe her memory is better than mine."

"Except if *she* remembered *you* from someplace, wouldn't she have mentioned it?"

"You're right, most likely she would have. I guess my mind was just playing a trick on me."

Elizabeth reflected on the character of Mrs. Mueller. On the one hand, she was remarkably gracious and kind to her guests. But Katya could testify that there was a harder, darker side to her personality. *A trick . . . or a mystery?* wondered Elizabeth. *Who is Tatiana Mueller?*

* * *

Elizabeth, Jessica, Chris, and Alex played a doubles tennis match after dinner, and then Elizabeth and Chris stole off alone for a walk. Elizabeth thought briefly about Todd: Was he at home by the phone, waiting for her to call? She hoped not. She didn't want to feel guilty about having such a wonderful time with Chris . . . she wanted to savor the magic of the moment. After all, this was just a week's vacation, one week out of time. Soon enough she'd be returning to her real life in Sweet Valley. . . .

Chris took her hand and swung it lightly. "Penny for your thoughts," he said.

Elizabeth pushed Todd from her mind. Another subject rose in his place. "The white building we saw today," she said, "when we were playing Frisbee golf. I think Mrs. Mueller yelled at Katya for taking us there. What is it?"

In the moonlight she saw Chris lift his broad shoulders. "I have no idea," he said, his tone casual and unworried. "It's off-limits to staff, but I don't know anything else about it."

"Hmm." Elizabeth studied his profile. For a split second something about his glib answer gave her the impression that he was lying. Immediately she chided herself for being so oversuspicious. *I'm letting my imagination run away with me,* she realized. *I'm making a mystery where there isn't one. If Chris says he doesn't know anything about the white building, then he doesn't.*

As Chris turned to face her, putting his arms around her and gazing down into her face with warm, honest eyes, Elizabeth was even more certain that her momentary impression had been mistaken. She closed her eyes and felt his lips meet hers in a passionate kiss. No, she could trust Chris—she *did* trust Chris. She could tell by the way he held her so tenderly that he didn't have anything to hide. . . .

Half an hour later Elizabeth said a reluctant good night to Chris and wandered back to Tranquillity Cottage. Mrs. Wakefield and Mrs. Fowler had retired for the night; Enid was in bed with a book; Lila was soaking in the hot tub; Jessica was lounging in the living area, contemplating the directory of spa services.

"Liz, you have grass in your hair," Jessica said with a smirk when her sister sat down next to her on the couch.

Elizabeth put a hand to her head, smiling sheepishly. She and Chris had sat down for a while on a secluded patch of lawn to look at the stars. . . . "Do I?"

Jessica laughed. "I am really shocked, Liz. You used to be such a good girl. What's happened to you?"

"This is completely innocent," Elizabeth protested. "Chris and I are just—" Realizing she didn't have a very good defense, she went on the offense to compensate. "Well, what about you and Alex?"

"Why pretend? We're falling madly in love," Jessica declared, dimpling. "Then again, maybe it's all a dream, a figment of my imagination. Alex is just too sweet and cute to be true. Isn't this whole *place* too good to be true?"

Elizabeth sank back against the couch, suddenly pensive. "Maybe . . . maybe not," she replied. "I mean, on the surface I agree—everything seems perfect. But then there are things like the really strict rules for the staff about not leaving the grounds, even on their day off. And what about that white building? Something's definitely up with Katya. And you know who else is acting incredibly weird? Enid."

"Weird in what way?"

Elizabeth tried to put her finger on it. "She's getting so serious about all this spa stuff, and Mrs. Mueller's paying a lot of extra attention to her. It's like she's trying to convert her or something."

Jessica shrugged. "It's totally natural, if you ask me. Enid just wants to be beautiful—that's why we're here, right?"

"So you don't think there's something strange about Paradise Spa?" asked Elizabeth.

"Not at all," said Jessica. Reaching out, she gave her sister's arm a playful shake. "Don't fight it, Liz.

This is a once-in-a-lifetime opportunity—be like Enid and let yourself go. Paradise Spa is a place where dreams come true." Her eyes shone with conviction. "Beauty, love . . . It will happen for you, too, if you let it!"

Chapter 8

After breakfast on Tuesday, Alice went for a stroll around the lavishly landscaped gardens of Paradise Spa. When she spotted Katya, who'd just finished her morning shift in the dining room, Alice waved.

Katya crossed the lawn to join her. "Mrs. Wakefield, hi," she said with obvious pleasure. "Are you enjoying this beautiful morning?"

"I certainly am." Mrs. Wakefield gestured at a lush tangle of flowering fruit trees. "I feel like I'm walking in the Garden of Eden."

Katya's smile didn't quite reach her eyes. "Yes, this *is* Paradise," she said quietly. "But you should still watch your step. Even the Garden of Eden had its serpent."

Mrs. Wakefield studied Katya's pensive face. "Katya, I hope you won't mind, but Elizabeth told me about your . . . situation. That you'd run away from home. And I just want you to know that if you need someone to talk to . . ."

She let her sentence trail off; she didn't want to push. But Katya was eager to meet her halfway. "Oh, Mrs. Wakefield," she said, her eyes sparkling with tears, "you don't know how much it means to me to hear you say that. You see"—she blushed a faint, endearing pink—"you remind me of my own mother. I felt that right away when you arrived at the spa with your daughters. It's not so much the way you look as the way you are with them—when you talk together, and laugh together. . . ." Katya reached into her pocket for a tissue, then blew her nose discreetly.

Side by side they walked across the lawn toward a bench next to a bank of flowers. "Katya," Alice said gently, "I know I'm prying, but since we're having a heart-to-heart . . . It's clear that you and your mother were—are—very close. Why did you run away from her?"

Katya sat down on the bench with a tired sigh. "For many years, after my father's death, it was just me, my older brother, and Mom," she explained, gazing off into the distance. "Then Mom remarried. Her new husband . . ." Katya shrugged. "He's OK. I mean, he was never actually mean to me—it wasn't anything he said or did. But I could tell he didn't want me around. My brother was in college at that point, so he wasn't an issue. It was just me—I was the one in the way."

"I'm sure your mother didn't think you were in the way!" said Mrs. Wakefield.

"Well, she never said anything to make me feel we were still a family, that I still counted," Katya said, tearful again. "I felt totally left out of the picture. Leaving seemed like the only thing to do."

Mrs. Wakefield squeezed Katya's arm. "It sounds like it was tough. Having a new stepfather—that's a big change. But remember, *he* had to adjust to you, too. Maybe if you'd given it a little time, or if you'd talked to your mother about your worries . . ."

"I know." Katya's voice sank to a barely audible whisper. "I acted on impulse—it was a mistake."

"The good thing is, it's a mistake you can fix," Alice declared. "Why don't you go home, Katya? I'm sure your mother *and* your stepfather would welcome you back with open arms."

Katya shook her head. "I can't go home. Mrs. Mueller wouldn't—Mrs. Mueller relies on me. I can't leave this job."

"Of course you can," said Alice. "Mrs. Mueller would understand."

But Katya continued to shake her head almost mechanically. "I can't go home," she repeated, a tremble in her voice. "I already told Elizabeth—I can't go home again, ever."

Mrs. Wakefield was mystified, but she decided

not to press the point. "Promise me this, then," she said, shifting tactics. "Will you at least phone your mother? Reopen the lines of commuication, tell her where you are and that you're all right?"

As she spoke, Alice gazed earnestly into Katya's sad eyes. For a long moment Katya just stared at her. Then she nodded, a tentative smile curving her lips. "OK," she agreed at last. "I'll think about it."

Alice realized this was the best she was going to get, at least today. She squeezed Katya's hand. "I'm glad."

Katya stood up. "I have to be going," she said. "I'll see you around. Have a nice day, Mrs. Wakefield."

She took a step away and then turned back. Bending, she planted a light, swift kiss on Alice's cheek. Then she darted off across the grass like a deer in flight from hunters.

Alice tilted her head thoughtfully. "That poor lost child," she murmured to herself. "I hope she makes that telephone call. As beautiful as it is, Paradise Spa isn't a substitute for a home and family."

Rising, she walked toward the pool, where she planned to swim a few laps before yoga class. In the distance she saw Katya pause before entering the building; the girl exchanged a few words with Mrs. Mueller, who was on her way out. When she spotted Alice, Mrs. Mueller made a beeline in her direction.

For some reason Alice felt uncomfortable

around Tatiana Mueller; she'd half hoped the other woman wouldn't notice her, but now escape was impossible. "Alice, how delightful to see you," Mrs. Mueller crooned. "And may I venture to say that, if possible, you are looking even more vibrant and lovely than on the day you arrived at Paradise. The veritable picture of health."

Alice smiled weakly. "Tell that to my aching muscles!" she joked.

"Ah, yes." Mrs. Mueller peered at her closely. "You're a living, breathing advertisement for the healthful benefits of the spa. If only we could keep you here forever!"

"We're enjoying the vacation, but by the end of the week I think we'll be ready to go home," Alice remarked. "There's always next year—maybe we'll come back."

Mrs. Mueller nodded. "Of course, of course. Yes, I certainly hope you will. Now I must be off—I have an appointment."

"Just one thing, before you go," said Alice.

Mrs. Mueller cocked her head, birdlike. "Yes?"

"I've been wondering if there's any chance that you and I have met before."

A strange smile flitted across Mrs. Mueller's face. "Ah. I seem familiar to you?"

"Vaguely," Alice said. She laughed uneasily, suddenly wishing she'd never raised the subject. "But I can't quite place you—you know how it is."

Mrs. Mueller continued to smile enigmatically. "Of course."

She still hadn't answered Alice's question. "So," said Alice. "Childhood? Or college, perhaps?"

"I spent my childhood in Europe," said Mrs. Mueller, "and came to the United States for university. But I don't believe we studied at the same school."

"Sweet Valley University?"

Mrs. Mueller shook her head. "No."

"And you've never lived or done business near Sweet Valley."

Mrs. Mueller lifted her hands in a gesture of apology. "I'm sorry. I think it is a case of . . . mistaken identity."

"Yes, that must be it." Mrs. Wakefield felt relieved; the nagging question had been settled. "Well, I'm off to the pool to loosen up before yoga," she said.

"Enjoy, enjoy," Mrs. Mueller urged.

"I will," promised Alice.

She strolled off, unaccountably glad to part with Mrs. Mueller. Even as she walked quickly away, however, Alice could still feel the other woman's overpowering presence. She knew that if she turned around suddenly, she'd catch Mrs. Mueller staring after her.

"Already we see an improvement, do we not?"

Seated in a chair in one of the Paradise Spa

salons, Enid smiled up at Mrs. Mueller. "Everyone tells me I look different."

"Yes." Mrs. Mueller plucked at a strand of Enid's hair. "It is more silky and pliant. And your skin . . ." She peered closely at Enid's face. "The complexion is smoother, more translucent. A few more treatments, and the freckles will be only a memory."

Enid laughed. "I wouldn't have thought that was possible, but Paradise Spa is making me believe in miracles."

"Yes." Mrs. Mueller smiled. "That is the true nature of my business: performing miracles, large and small—transformations of the outer person and the inner spirit. So today I will apply your facial treatment, is that acceptable? Wilhelmina's schedule is full."

"Of course," said Enid, flattered that Mrs. Mueller would go to so much trouble for her. "Thanks—thanks so much."

Reclining in the chair, she closed her eyes. After cleansing Enid's face, Mrs. Mueller carefully applied the thick, pungent lotion. Enid felt her skin begin to tingle. "Now, as you did at your first treatment, you must stay in this position for twenty minutes," Mrs. Mueller instructed. "And we can talk; or, rather, since your facial muscles should remain still, I will talk and you may listen."

Enid gave a slight nod to indicate that this was fine. "Ah," said Mrs. Mueller, "isn't it a pleasure to be pampered? Just like when you were a baby."

The lulling cadences of Mrs. Mueller's musical voice wrapped around Enid; she felt her entire body relax. "Think back, Enid," Mrs. Mueller instructed. "Think back to childhood. We'll walk together through the years, growing younger and younger at each step. You are sixteen now, no? Remember fifteen. Fourteen. Thirteen, the year you became a teenager. We are moving through time—can you feel the years dropping away while the memories come alive?"

Enid's head felt light; her body seemed to be floating above the reclining chair. It was like being on the verge of sleep, but at the same time she was preternaturally aware of certain things: the air moving in and out of her lungs, the cool, stinging lotion on her face, and above all things, Mrs. Mueller's voice.

"You remember junior high school, don't you?" Mrs. Mueller was saying. "The time when a young girl begins to blossom into a woman. You felt awkward and plain, not as pretty as many of your friends. There was a boy you liked very much, but he preferred another girl. You wondered if you would ever be attractive to the opposite sex, and your mother . . . your mother taunted you. She said no, no boy could love you because you were ugly."

Even in her hypnotized state Enid struggled with this last image. *Mom taunted me? Called me ugly? Did that really happen? But it must have,* she decided mournfully. *These are my memories.*

"In high school," Mrs. Mueller resumed, "you did begin to date and have boyfriends. But the relationships never lasted. The boys always left you for other, prettier girls, didn't they? And all the time you had to watch your best friend, Elizabeth, and her twin sister, Jessica, reign supreme on the social scene by virtue of their beauty and popularity. Worst of all, Elizabeth had a loving relationship with her doting mother, while your own mother continued to neglect you. Gradually, your resentment of Elizabeth turned inward and you began to hate yourself."

Briefly, ineffectually, Enid fought against this suggestion. She resented Elizabeth? She hated herself? *Yes, I must,* she concluded at last. *Liz is beautiful, beloved, and I'm not. How could it be otherwise?*

"You hate yourself," Mrs. Mueller repeated. "And you want to be different. You want to change your appearance—body, complexion, hair, nose, chin, cheekbones—so that your outer person is as beautiful as the person within, so that you finally get the affection and admiration you deserve. Now, Enid, come back to the present moment. Come back to me."

Slowly, the haze of painful memories cleared from Enid's head. Feeling as if she were waking from a restless sleep, she realized that Mrs.

Mueller was gently wiping the lotion from her face and patting her skin with a damp cloth. "Did you doze?" Mrs. Mueller asked. "Did you dream?"

Enid blinked her eyes. She looked straight up at Mrs. Mueller, a desperate, hopeful light in her eyes. "I want to be a different person," she whispered. "Can you help me?"

A triumphant smile wreathed Mrs. Mueller's misshapen face. "Of course I can help you, my dear," she asserted. "There is an operation that can change your whole life and outlook for the better. Let me tell you about it. . . ."

"Katya, wait up!" Elizabeth was crossing the lobby of the main building, en route from the tennis courts to the steam room. Spying Katya, she hurried over to say hello.

Katya turned. "Did you have a nice tennis lesson?" she asked with a stiff smile.

Elizabeth nodded. "I picked up some really good tips. I could see the improvement right away, especially in my backhand."

"That's nice," said Katya.

Elizabeth got the feeling Katya was getting ready to take off. She placed a hand on her arm. "Mom told me you two talked—I'm really glad," said Elizabeth. "Have you had a chance to call your mother yet?"

Katya took a step away from Elizabeth so that Elizabeth had to drop her hand. Her artificial smile remained fixed in place. "I've been so happy since I came to work at Paradise Spa," Katya said. "It's such a great lifestyle—the environment is healthful and beautiful, I have good friends and many benefits, I'm learning about the spa business—I have everything I could ever want or need. I never want to leave—I consider this my home now."

Elizabeth looked at Katya in confusion. *What is she talking about? Why didn't she answer my question about calling her mother?*

Then Elizabeth saw Katya's eyes dart nervously toward the reception desk. Following Katya's gaze, Elizabeth realized that Mrs. Mueller was standing nearby, watching Katya with a hawklike expression.

She overheard our entire conversation, Elizabeth realized. *Is that why Katya's acting like this—she doesn't want Mrs. Mueller to find out that she's thinking of getting in touch with her family and leaving Paradise Spa?*

As Katya continued to ramble on about what a wonderful opportunity it was to live and work at Paradise Spa, Elizabeth noticed that the other girl's hands were clenched in tight, tense fists. There was no doubt about it: Katya was scared. *Why?* wondered Elizabeth. *Is she just worried about making another mistake and getting fired, or is there something else going on?*

"I can't eat another bite," Enid declared at dinner.

Elizabeth glanced at her friend's plate. The portions were small to begin with, and half of Enid's meal was untouched. "That's all you're going to eat?" Elizabeth asked in disbelief. "You mean you're not ravenous like the rest of us?"

Enid patted her waist. "I'm trying to lose those extra pounds I put on recently. I've always wanted to have a figure more like yours, Liz."

Enid took a small envelope from the pocket of her cardigan sweater. Ripping it open, she removed a pill. Elizabeth watched her swallow the pill with a glass of water. "What was that?" she asked.

"A vitamin supplement," Enid explained. "Mrs. Mueller gave it to me. They're specially formulated for freckled redheads to improve hair and skin tone. I'm supposed to take one with each meal."

In all the information provided about the spa's services, Elizabeth couldn't remember reading anything about vitamin treatments. "Do you think that's smart?" she asked. "I mean, to take special vitamins without a doctor's prescribing them?"

Enid laughed. "Liz, this is a health spa! I have complete faith in Mrs. Mueller—she wouldn't recommend something that wasn't safe and beneficial." Patting her lips with a napkin, Enid pushed back her chair. "I'm off to the gym," she said brightly. "Thought I'd squeeze in one last workout. See you back at the room!"

Enid strolled off with bouncing, energetic steps. Elizabeth turned back to her dinner, her forehead wrinkled. It was great to see her friend feeling so good, but at the same time, she couldn't help being a tiny bit concerned. *Enid eats only half her dinner, and then she runs off for one last workout. And what's with the special vitamins for redheads?*

Elizabeth's train of thought was interrupted by an exclamation from Lila. "There he is!" Lila burst out. "I haven't seen him all day. This is it." Lila tossed her napkin onto the table. "I have to meet him—I can't hold back any longer."

"What are you going to say to him?" asked Jessica.

Lila shrugged. "I'll say something like, 'I notice you're dining alone and I wondered if you'd like some company.'" She fluttered her thick black eyelashes. "It's not what I say, though, it's how I say it. Wish me luck!"

The twins watched Lila stride purposefully across the dining room in the direction of the mystery man's table. At the same time, Katya was crossing the room with a heavily laden tray.

Both girls were so intent on their goals that they didn't see each other until it was too late. Jessica saw the collision coming and covered her eyes. There was a loud crash of dishes breaking; somebody shrieked. "Ouch!" said Jessica. "I can't look. Is it as bad as I think?"

Elizabeth grimaced. "Picture the *Titanic* hitting the iceberg. Total disaster!"

Peeking out from between her fingers, Jessica saw Lila, her hair and her white dress covered with food, Katya on her hands and knees picking up the debris from her tray, and Lila's mystery man making a hasty exit.

"Poor Lila," said Jessica with a giggle as her friend stomped out, apparently on her way back to the cottage to shower and change. "She is doomed never to meet that man!"

Two other waitresses were helping clean up the mess; Katya hurried to the kitchen with a tray of broken dishes. Even from a distance Elizabeth could tell she was crying. "Poor Katya," she said softly.

Enid breezed into the cottage later that evening. "Hi, Liz. What's up? Aren't you going out with Chris tonight?"

Elizabeth was curled on the sofa in the living room; she looked up from her book when Enid entered the room. "He needed to spend an hour or two doing inventory at the pro shop," she replied, "but we're meeting later for a walk."

After grabbing a bottle of mineral water from the refrigerator, Enid dropped into a chair facing Elizabeth. "I'm really pooped," she declared, "but it feels good."

"I can't believe how hard you're working yourself!"

"The pounds are melting away." Enid beamed. "Pretty soon I'll weigh the same as you!"

Elizabeth laughed. "I don't think I'm necessarily the standard. Everyone's different, you know?

What's right for me might not be right for somebody else."

"Well, I know exactly how I'd like to look," said Enid, her eyes glittering with intensity, "and I'm on the right track. I can feel it."

Elizabeth closed her book and looked solemnly at her friend. "Enid," she began, after a moment's hesitation, "don't you think that maybe you're starting to take this 'beautiful person within' thing a little too seriously? I mean, coming to the spa was supposed to be fun, a lark. . . ."

Enid narrowed her eyes. "What do you mean, 'too seriously'?"

"The vitamins, the facials and hair treatments, the compulsive exercise . . . and practically starving yourself at meals." Elizabeth shrugged helplessly. "It's just not like you to go overboard with this kind of stuff."

"What's really bothering you, Liz?" demanded Enid, her temper flaring. "Don't you want me to be as beautiful as you are?"

"Enid!" exclaimed Elizabeth. "I can't believe you said that. It's not like that at all!"

"Then why aren't you supporting me? Can't you see how much this means to me?"

Elizabeth took a deep breath; she wanted to make sure she chose her words carefully. "What I see is . . . that you've been kind of depressed lately because of what happened with Hugh, and you think that you'll be happier if you change how you look. But in my opinion—and I'm only offering it because I care about you—you're beautiful just the way you are."

Enid shook her head. "You just don't understand," she insisted. "You've always been the prettiest girl in town. All I want is a chance to get the kind of attention you and Jessica take for granted. Is that so bad?"

"No, but . . ." Elizabeth felt as if she were banging her head against a wall—she wasn't getting her point across. "Getting attention because of the way you look is a mixed blessing, if you ask me. It doesn't build *real* self-esteem. Being pretty doesn't automatically solve your problems—happiness has to come from inside."

Enid rose to her feet. "Sorry we're not seeing eye to eye," she said stiffly. "I guess you'll just have to do your thing at Paradise, and I'll do mine."

Before Elizabeth could reply, Enid stalked into the bedroom and closed the door. With a sigh Elizabeth reopened her novel. But she couldn't focus on reading. Enid's accusation hovered in the air: *"Don't you want me to be as beautiful as you are?"*

"That's not it!" Elizabeth repeated out loud, still indignant. She and Enid had never been competitive—their friendship wasn't like Lila's and Jessica's, based on rivalry. *Is it me?* Elizabeth wondered. *Am* I *behaving differently?* No, she decided. Enid was the one going through some kind of personality transformation. It wasn't like her to be so prickly and defensive, or so obsessed with her appearance.

Closing her book again, Elizabeth tossed it aside in frustration. She hadn't intended to pick a fight with Enid. *Maybe I should've just kept my mouth shut,* she thought. She recalled her conversation with Jessica the night before. "This is a place where dreams come true. Enid's got the right idea—she's not fighting the magic. It will happen for you, too, if you let it. . . ."

Speaking of magic . . . Elizabeth looked at her watch. Pushing her worries about Enid from her mind, she headed out to find Chris.

Jessica hummed softly to herself as she and Lila strolled across the shadowy grounds of Paradise Spa. Jessica had talked Lila into coming with her for a quick swim before she met Alex in the steam room. She was wearing her sexy new white bikini with a flowered pareu tied in a knot at her slender waist—she couldn't wait to see Alex's expression when she walked into the steam room. "He won't need any steam to make his temperature shoot through the ceiling!" she anticipated cheerfully.

"Great," said Lila, rolling her eyes. "I'm so glad I'll be here to observe."

The night air was fragrant and cool; Jessica shivered, quickening her steps. Ahead, next to an illuminated swimming pool that shone like an aquamarine jewel in the night, she glimpsed the shingle cottage housing the steam room. "You go ahead and take a dip," she said to Lila. "I'm going to see if Alex is here yet."

"Alex?" she called, as Lila dived into the pool.

There was no answer. *Maybe he's late, or waiting for me inside,* she thought.

She pushed open the door. The lighting in the steam room was muted; Jessica stepped into a thick cloud of warm mist. "Alex?" she called again. "Is anyone here?"

The only answer was the hissing of the steam.

For some reason, even though the air around her was now warm, Jessica continued to shiver. The deserted steam room was eerie, the fingers of mist ghostlike. Jessica made her way toward one of the cedar benches that lined the wall.

Then the steam parted; she caught a glimpse of a dark, crumpled form lying half on the bench and half on the floor. "Alex?" Jessica cried for the third time, her heart in her throat.

There was no response; the figure was still, silent.

Fearfully, Jessica drew nearer. *It's not a body,* she told herself, her teeth chattering. *It can't be a body.*

It *was* a body. It was a girl with long black hair, leaning against the bench as if she were asleep. Jessica couldn't see her face, but she knew who it was. *Katya! Maybe she's just asleep,* Jessica thought hopefully.

She stepped closer and reached out a shaking hand. "Katya?"

Silence.

Her hand shaking, Jessica gingerly touched Katya's shoulder. The girl's body fell back limply, revealing her face. The green eyes were wide open, staring blindly at the ceiling. Blind eyes . . . dead eyes.

Jessica jumped away from the corpse, a scream of terror bubbling up in her throat. As she turned and ran out of the steam room, she was screaming as if she would never stop.

Chapter 9

Elizabeth and Chris were walking hand in hand across the moonlit golf course when they heard a piercing scream in the distance. They stopped dead in their tracks and looked at each other with wide, startled eyes. The scream was repeated—a girl's voice, high-pitched with horror. Someone was in terrible trouble!

"It came from over there, back at the spa!" said Chris.

Elizabeth was already in motion. "Come on," she cried. "Let's go!"

They sprinted down the hill past the pro shop and the tennis courts, following the sound of the screams. As they neared the swimming pool, Elizabeth pointed to their source. "Look, by the steam room. It's Jessica!"

Mrs. Wakefield, Lila, Enid, the Randall family,

and a few employees also drawn by Jessica's cries were hurrying toward the steam room. Jessica was no longer screaming, but her body was racked with sobs. She stood with her face in her hands, leaning against Alex for support.

"Jessica, what's the matter?" said Elizabeth, rushing to her sister's side.

Jessica couldn't speak. She lifted her face, streaked with tears, and nodded toward the door to the steam room. "In—in there," she stuttered. "Katya. She's d-dead."

Elizabeth gasped. Katya . . . dead! In three steps Elizabeth was at the door to the steam room, which stood slightly ajar. Someone intercepted her just as she was about to step through the door.

Mrs. Mueller lifted an arm, as if to block Elizabeth's entrance. "Let me," she croaked, her voice rough.

Elizabeth had no choice but to step aside and allow Mrs. Mueller to precede her into the steam room. Because Jessica had left the door open, the steam had for the most part cleared. Katya's prone body was visible immediately.

Mrs. Mueller rushed across the room and knelt next to the dead girl. Elizabeth hurried after her. "Don't touch the body," she called. "The police should be the first to examine her, in case there are any clues about who killed her!"

"Who killed her?" Mrs. Mueller rose to her feet and stepped aside so that Elizabeth could view the corpse. "No one killed her. Do you see any signs of a struggle?"

Elizabeth forced herself to look down at Katya's lifeless body. Tears welled up in her eyes as she stared at her friend's pale, unconscious face—lips that would never smile again, eyes that would never see.

"Do you see any blood to indicate that she was attacked?" Mrs. Mueller pressed. "Any marks on her throat, any bruises?"

"No," said Elizabeth. "No, I don't."

"Neither do I. She looks almost . . . peaceful." Mrs. Mueller clucked her tongue sadly. "Poor young thing. You know, she had a serious heart condition. She shouldn't have been in here, where the heat could raise her blood pressure to a dangerous level. No, it wasn't foul play. I fear she suffered a lapse of judgment that cost her her life."

"Katya had a heart condition?" Elizabeth said, surprised. "You're kidding. I can't believe . . ."

Her voice trailed off as other people crowded into the steam room. There were shocked exclamations and sobs from Katya's friends on the Paradise Spa staff. Elizabeth stepped aside, pondering Mrs. Mueller's revelation. Katya had a heart condition . . . she shouldn't have been in the steam room. . . . It just didn't sound right. In fact, if anything, Elizabeth had formed the opposite impression of Katya's health. She'd seemed to be in exceptional physical shape—Elizabeth had barely been able to keep pace with her on the uphill run to the waterfall a few mornings ago.

She was so strong, so vibrant, so young . . . and now she's dead. A shudder traveled through Elizabeth's body. How could something like this have happened?

While she found it hard to believe that Katya had had a fatal heart condition, Elizabeth leaned toward agreeing with Mrs. Mueller on one thing. *Katya must have died from natural causes,* Elizabeth reasoned. *Who on earth would want to kill her?*

Mrs. Mueller's assistant, Marguerite, appeared and began clearing people out of the steam room. "I've phoned the ambulance," she informed Mrs. Mueller. "It should be here any minute now."

One friend of Katya's, the waitress named Lulu, was too overcome with shock and grief to budge. She stood over Katya's body, sobbing inconsolably.

"There, there, dear," Mrs. Mueller murmured, patting Lulu's shoulder. "I'm afraid there's nothing you can do for her now. Here, dry your eyes and go back inside with the others."

Mrs. Mueller reached into her pocket. She pulled out a tissue to hand to Lulu, and as she did, a small piece of paper flew out of her pocket and fluttered to the ground. Elizabeth bent to retrieve it for her, but before her fingers could close around the note, Mrs. Mueller snatched it up and stuck it back into her pocket.

Elizabeth straightened up, intentionally keeping her expression blank. Mrs. Mueller had struck as swiftly as a snake, but not so swiftly that Elizabeth didn't get a good look at the scrap of paper.

It was a handwritten note, and she'd had time to read only the first line: "Mrs. Wakefield, please meet me in the steam room. . . ." Elizabeth's pulse was racing; questions crowded her brain. Why did Mrs. Mueller have a note addressed to Mrs. Wakefield? Who was it from? Elizabeth had a strong hunch she knew the answer to the second question. She would have bet anything that Katya had written the note, but Mrs. Mueller had intercepted it somehow. On purpose or by accident? Was this significant?

Elizabeth cast a final, sorrowful glance at Katya's lifeless form. *She was scared of something . . . or someone . . . at Paradise Spa,* Elizabeth thought, remembering Katya's odd behavior in recent days. *She wanted to talk to Mom again, to tell her something. It must have been important. What was it, and why didn't Mrs. Mueller want her to?*

Elizabeth feared she'd never learn the answers to these questions. Because the person who held the key to the mystery was dead.

"I can't believe she's really dead," Jessica said to Alex. "I can't believe this afternoon she was fine, and now . . . And the worst thing is, she's *our* age." She put her hands to her face, overcome by the thought. "How could someone so young just *die*?"

She and Alex were alone in the room he shared with Chris, sitting on the couch. Jessica was still trembling from head to toe. Alex put his arm around her and rubbed her shoulder gently. "It's terrible," he agreed. "I'm sorry you had to be the one to find her body."

Jessica wiped her eyes with a tissue. "I'll never forget that moment. It's imprinted on my brain forever. But this is probably harder for you. I mean, you knew her better than I did."

Alex shrugged. "I really didn't know her that well."

"But you worked with her. Aren't you really upset about this?"

"Sure," said Alex. "Of course I'm upset. Everyone is."

Jessica looked at him. He didn't *sound* upset. "You're acting like this isn't that big a deal," she observed, sniffling. "Like dead bodies turn up in the steam room every day!"

Alex laughed uncomfortably. "Don't be ridiculous. I agree with you—it's awful, a tragedy. Katya was too young to die. But . . ."

"But what?"

"But nothing," said Alex. "Maybe I . . . maybe I should just walk you back to the cottage."

"Are you trying to get rid of me?" she asked, hurt.

Alex stroked her hair. "Of course not. But I bet

your mother and sister are worried about you. I know you're all worked up, but probably the best thing for you to do is try to get some sleep."

"OK," said Jessica reluctantly.

"You'll see," said Alex. "This will be easier in the morning—we'll still be grieving over Katya, but everything won't seem so scary and confusing."

Jessica gazed deep into Alex's dark-brown eyes, a tiny seed of uncertainty blossoming in her heart. What was it about him tonight that seemed a little . . . off? He'd rocked her in his arms and said all the right things to comfort her, but somehow his words and his embrace felt detached, mechanical. *As if he really has no feelings about this, about Katya's death, at all,* Jessica realized. *It didn't shake him up in the least.*

Alex bent his head to kiss her, and as always the kiss was delicious. Alex was a great kisser; Alex was great at everything he did. *He's perfect,* Jessica thought, but for the first time this struck her as a character flaw. He was so close to perfect, he almost seemed less than human. . . .

"So, Mom, you have no idea what Katya might have wanted to talk to you about?" Elizabeth asked Alice back in the cottage later that evening.

Mrs. Wakefield shook her head tiredly. "She didn't say anything, and I didn't receive a note from her."

"That's because Mrs. Mueller had the note. She stole it!"

"Honey, I think you're being a little melodramatic," said Mrs. Wakefield. "My guess is that Katya dropped the note, and Mrs. Mueller planned to return it to her. Something harmless like that."

Elizabeth was unconvinced. "Maybe. But the fact is, Mom, Katya went to the steam room to meet you and she ended up dead."

"Of heart failure," Mrs. Wakefield reminded Elizabeth.

"We don't know that for sure," Elizabeth countered.

Alice sighed. "You're right. We don't. But Mrs. Mueller seems certain that that's what happened. And she was familiar with Katya's health status—Katya was her employee." Putting a hand to her mouth, Mrs. Wakefield stifled a yawn. "Honey, I'm going to bed. I'll see you in the morning, OK?"

"OK," said Elizabeth glumly.

Alice moved closer to Elizabeth so she could put her arms around her. "I know how you feel," she said softly. "I cared about Katya, too."

Elizabeth rested her head against her mother's shoulder for a moment. "Thanks, Mom."

Mrs. Wakefield disappeared into her and Mrs. Fowler's bedroom. A moment later the light went out. The light was also out in Jessica and Lila's room.

Enid was still awake, reading in bed. Elizabeth stuck her head into the bedroom. "Enid, I'm going to take a little walk," she said. "I need some fresh air. I won't be long, but you don't have to wait up for me."

Enid nodded. "Take care, Liz."

After retrieving he small flashlight from her purse and putting it in her pocket, Elizabeth stepped out into the night. *Take care. . . .* She shivered. Had Katya died of natural causes, or did danger prowl the darkness? *If she didn't have heart failure, then someone killed her,* thought Elizabeth. *Someone who's still here at Paradise Spa. . . .*

Elizabeth didn't have a particular destination in mind, but all at once she realized her footsteps were leading her in the direction of the small building where Katya had lived with other members of the kitchen staff. Elizabeth studied the dark windows, trying to remember which had been Katya's. *The second from the left, I think,* she decided, stepping into the foyer. Yes, of course—there was Katya's name on the door.

She tiptoed across the foyer and put her hand on the doorknob, expecting it to be locked. Instead the knob turned in her hand. Elizabeth caught her breath; suddenly her heart was beating like a drum. She knew what she had to do, though. She pushed the door open, slipped into the room, and shut the door silently behind her.

The room was pitch-black. Turning on her flashlight, Elizabeth held her fingers over the bulb and pointed it at the floor, so the light wouldn't be seen from outside. *The door was open—I'm not really breaking in,* she told herself as she crossed the room. *And besides, Katya wouldn't mind. I'm doing this for her.*

Suddenly Elizabeth understood what had drawn her there. No matter what her mother might say, she wasn't satisfied with Mrs. Mueller's heart-failure theory. Katya had been the picture of health—it simply didn't make sense. No, somebody had killed Katya—Elizabeth was almost certain of it. The question was who—and why?

Maybe there will be a clue here, among Katya's belongings, Elizabeth thought, shining the flashlight around the room.

The room was small, furnished only with a bed, nightstand, dresser, writing desk, and chair. Thinking that her desk at home harbored most of her own secrets, Elizabeth went there first. On top of the desk there was a pad of paper and a pen. Elizabeth ruffled the sheets—all were blank. *But it could be the pad Katya wrote the note on,* Elizabeth speculated. The only other object on top of the desk was a small framed photograph. Elizabeth directed the flashlight onto it. It was a picture of a woman with dark hair. There was no strong resemblance to Katya, but nevertheless, Elizabeth was sure that the woman in the photo was Katya's mother.

One by one, Elizabeth opened the desk drawers. She found a few paperback novels and an empty vitamin bottle. "Nothing," Elizabeth murmured aloud to herself.

As she replaced the novels, one of them slipped from her fingers. Picking it up, Elizabeth noticed a piece of folded paper that had apparently been used as a bookmark. She removed the paper and unfolded it.

It was half of a page torn from a magazine. "Help-wanted ads," noted Elizabeth. "Hmm . . . maybe Katya was looking for a new job." Then Elizabeth spotted the large advertisement. It was for Paradise Spa!

"WANT TO BE BEAUTIFUL?" asked the ad in large, eye-catching print. "Spend the summer working in a luxurious spa while you partake of all we have to offer."

So this is how Katya found out about Paradise, Elizabeth surmised, turning over the scrap of paper. The name of the magazine was printed on the bottom left-hand corner: *Manford House,* a publication Elizabeth had never heard of.

Elizabeth wasn't sure it would prove to be important, but she folded up the paper and put it in her pocket anyway. A cursory search of the rest of the room and bathroom turned up nothing but clothing and toiletries—no letters, no journal, no other snapshots. *She didn't bring much with her,* Elizabeth concluded, taking one last sad look around the room.

Katya had been a lonely, solitary girl—a runaway—and now she was dead. Would the spa even be able to track down her family? Would anyone mourn her?

I'll mourn her, Elizabeth vowed, her eyes filling with tears as she stepped into the foyer and closed the door to Katya's room. *And I'll get to the bottom of this mystery. I'll catch her murderer if it's the last thing I do!*

Elizabeth had not yet returned from her walk, and Enid was alone in the bedroom. Putting her book aside, Enid padded in bare feet to the dresser where she'd left her purse. Rummaging inside, she located her small compact.

She snapped open the compact and held up the mirror to study her face, taking stock of her features. *Reddish-brown hair, tends to curl. Green eyes. Skin fair, with freckles. Lips average, maybe a little on the thin side. Cheekbones nonexistent. And don't even get me started on my body!*

Yes, that's my face, the face I've had all my life, thought Enid. *The face I always figured I'd have to live with forever. . . .*

She held the mirror closer, squinting her eyes until the image blurred slightly. Now she imagined a different face, with elegant features, a flawless complexion, and a mane of hair any color or texture she desired. *My nose would be straight,* thought Enid. *I'd have cheekbones like a model. And good-bye, freckles!*

She felt nervous and excited; her heart bumped in her chest. Should she do it? Should she have the surgery Mrs. Mueller had suggested?

Would it really be the answer to all her problems?

Mrs. Mueller says I can be whoever I want, Enid thought, her eyes glowing with conviction. *Why should I let this boring old face stand in my way? Mom would never understand, but then again, she doesn't understand anything. She doesn't have the faintest idea how I feel, what I've been going through. Face it—she doesn't have the time, she doesn't care. But Mrs. Mueller does care.*

A warm rush of affection coursed through Enid's blood. Mrs. Mueller had been so kind! She considered Enid the daughter she'd never had—she really was genuinely concerned for her welfare. Yes, unlike Enid's own mother, Mrs. Mueller wanted her to be happy—that was her sole motivation in encouraging Enid to take such a drastic, life-altering step.

"I could do it," Enid said to the plain face in the mirror . . . the face she might not have to live with for much longer. "And then I might just decide to stay here at Paradise Spa. Maybe I'll never go back to Sweet Valley. . . ."

Chapter 10

On Wednesday morning the mood at the spa was subdued. By now everyone, both staff and guests, had heard about Katya's sudden and untimely death the night before. Someone—Lulu, Elizabeth suspected—had left a bouquet of flowers tied with a black ribbon lying on the concrete outside the steam room.

At breakfast the Sweet Valley group decided to start the day with an aerobics class. Only Elizabeth opted out. "I'll meet you later at the swimming pool," she told her mother and the others. "I think . . . I think I'd like to spend some quiet time in our room by myself, maybe do some writing."

Jessica gave her sister a sympathetic look; Mrs. Wakefield squeezed her daughter's hand.

Back in the cottage Elizabeth turned on her

portable computer. Plugging the modem into the phone line, she logged on.

After dialing Olivia Davidson's E-mail address at the newspaper office back at Sweet Valley High, Elizabeth typed a quick query, then sat back to wait for a response, her fingers crossed. Like Elizabeth, arts editor Olivia often stopped in the *Oracle* office even when school wasn't in session; with any luck Elizabeth would find her catching up on *Oracle* business now. "Please be there," Elizabeth muttered aloud.

A minute later her wish was granted. A message flashed on the screen: She had received some E-mail!

Elizabeth hit a few keys, "opening" her mail, and there was Olivia's reply, typed only seconds before. "I got your note, Liz," Olivia wrote, "and I'm looking up 'Manford House' on INFOMAX. Give me a minute, and I'll let you know what I find out about it."

Elizabeth drummed her fingers impatiently, picturing Olivia back at Sweet Valley High, signing onto INFOMAX and punching in her query. The newspaper staff used the database to do research for their articles—it gave them access to information published in newspapers and magazines all over the country. Elizabeth had even once used INFOMAX to solve the mystery of the true identity of a man Jessica had been dating—a man, it turned out, who made a living swindling women out of their money and property, and who was only using Jessica to advance a nefarious scheme.

Maybe INFOMAX will help me solve another mystery, Elizabeth hoped. *The mystery of Katya's life, and of her death. . . .*

It seemed like a century, but at last a second E-mail message arrived from Olivia. Elizabeth read it eagerly. "Manford House is a shelter for runaways—they have facilities in a bunch of midwestern and western states. The residents put out a monthly in-house magazine dealing with teen issues—it's circulated at Manford House shelters and also distributed to other places where troubled kids might look for help: clinics, youth centers, etc. By the way, Liz, you can access INFOMAX yourself long-distance by dialing your own *Oracle* account number. Let me know what's up, and if I can be of any more help, OK?"

Elizabeth typed a thank-you to Olivia and then turned off her computer. So Manford House was a shelter for runaways! Elizabeth already knew Katya had been a runaway—that was no surprise. The real revelation was that Katya had learned about the job opening at Paradise Spa through Manford House. *And if she did, maybe other staffers did, too,* Elizabeth deduced.

She sprang to her feet on a sudden hunch. A few minutes later she knocked on Chris's door.

"Liz!" he said, greeting her with a light kiss on

the cheek. "I was just on my way out. Walk me over to the golf course?"

"Sure," she said.

They headed down the path side by side. Elizabeth glanced at Chris's profile, wondering how to bring up the subject that was in her mind. She decided directness was the best approach. "Chris, I have to ask you a personal question."

He stopped in his tracks and looked down at her, his eyebrows slightly lifted. "What is it?" he asked, the expression in his eyes suddenly guarded.

Elizabeth put a hand on his arm and looked him straight in the face. "Are you a runaway?"

Chris jerked away from her touch as if he'd been jolted by an electric shock. For a moment he just stared at her without speaking; she could see that he was struggling with his answer . . . or whether to answer at all.

At last he sighed heavily. "Yeah, I'm a runaway," he admitted gruffly.

Elizabeth heard the note of shame in his voice. "You don't have to be embarrassed," she assured him. "You don't have to hide anything from me."

"I thought if you knew the truth, you might not . . . See, I've actually been at Paradise for three years, since I was sixteen. I didn't want to tell you that I never finished high school." He dropped his eyes. "I mean, because you're so smart, and I'm just a dropout."

"It doesn't matter to me," said Elizabeth. "I

don't think any less of you. I feel for you, though. It must have been tough, leaving home at sixteen and never going back. . . . Why did you do it?"

They were walking again. Chris kept his eyes directed straight ahead; his hands were pushed deep into the pockets of his shorts. "I was an abused kid," he said, his voice devoid of emotion. "As soon as I got old enough to take my life into my own hands, I split."

Elizabeth wiped a tear from her eye. Chris glanced at her and smiled crookedly. "Hey, it's not really such a tragedy," he said. "I ended up here, and believe me, this is a thousand times better than my life at home was. Mrs. Mueller has been like a parent to me—a real parent, a parent who builds you up instead of beating you up."

Elizabeth nodded sympathetically. "So how did you find out about Paradise Spa?"

She wasn't surprised to hear that Chris had read a help-wanted ad in a magazine similar to *Manford House*. "What about Alex?" she asked. "Is he a runaway, too? Did he find out about Paradise Spa in the same way?"

"Yep," said Chris. "His story is a lot like mine—pretty dismal, but with a happy ending." Suddenly Chris stopped and turned to Elizabeth, putting both hands on her arms. "Now you know my secret," he said. "Could you do me a favor, though? Could we not talk about this again? I've worked hard to put the past behind me. I want to live in the present moment—I don't like looking back."

"Sure," said Elizabeth. "I understand."

"Good." Chris brushed her cheek with a quick kiss. "I'm late, Liz—I've got to run. See you later, OK?"

With that he jogged off toward the pro shop. Elizabeth stared after him, her forehead creased in a puzzled frown. It had been a strangely dissatisfying conversation. On one hand, Chris had confided in her—she'd learned the truth about his past. On the other, as they'd ventured onto personal ground, Elizabeth had felt him retreating from her emotionally, holding her at arm's length, as if to say, "Watch your step—you can know this much about me, but no more."

I didn't even get to ask him what he thinks about the fact that so many of the people who work here are runaways, Elizabeth realized. As she walked back toward Tranquillity Cottage, though, she decided that maybe that wasn't a bad thing. Maybe she should keep her suspicions to herself until she knew what, if anything, they all added up to. . . .

Back at the cottage Enid was changing into a swimsuit and a cover-up. Elizabeth couldn't help noticing that she did look slimmer. "How was the aerobics class?" Elizabeth asked.

"Terrific," said Enid. "When we first got here, I could barely keep up with the instructor, but I'm getting a lot stronger. I'd like to do that myself someday—be an aerobics instructor, I mean. Wouldn't that be fun, getting paid to stay fit?"

Enid, an aerobics instructor? Elizabeth raised her eyebrows in astonishment. "You're kidding! You're not the type to—"

Just then the telephone in the living room rang. Elizabeth trotted out of the bedroom to pick it up. "Hello? Oh, hi, Mrs. Rollins! How are you? Yeah, we're having a blast. Hold on a minute—let me get her."

Enid was still in the bedroom. "Enid, it's your mom," Elizabeth called.

"I really don't have time to talk—I'm on my way out," Enid called back. "Tell her I'm not here."

Elizabeth put the phone down and went to the bedroom door. "Are you sure?" she asked, surprised.

Enid didn't meet Elizabeth's eyes. "I just don't feel like talking to her, OK?" she snapped.

Elizabeth returned to the phone, disconcerted. "Uh, Mrs. Rollins? She left a few seconds ago for a swim at the pool—you just missed her. But I'll tell her you called, all right? Great. See you soon. 'Bye."

Enid stood in the doorway, something like satisfaction on her face, and watched as Elizabeth hung up the phone. Elizabeth wanted to ask her friend what that was all about, refusing to take a phone call from her mother, but remembering Enid's sharp remark—*"I just don't feel like talking to her, OK?"*—she decided not to.

Instead Elizabeth presented her startling discovery about Paradise Spa to Enid. "I found this scrap of paper in a book in Katya's room," said Elizabeth, taking the help-wanted ad from her pocket. "She found out about this job while she was living at a shelter for runaways. And guess what? Chris just told me that he and Alex are both runaways, too! That's three people—too many to be a coincidence. Obviously Mrs. Mueller advertised in magazines like *Manford House* for a reason—she wanted to hire runaway kids. I bet the entire staff is made up of runaways! But why?"

Unlike Elizabeth, Enid didn't seem the least bit curious about or mystified by this development. "I don't think you need to turn it into some kind of conspiracy," she said, her expression sunny and untroubled. "In my opinion it's wonderful that Mrs. Mueller takes these homeless kids under her wing. She's such a caring person—she just loves to help people. What's the matter with that?"

Elizabeth was taken aback. "Well, when you put it that way . . ."

Enid stuck her bare feet into a pair of flip-flops. "I'm off to the pool. Will we see you over there?"

"Sure," said Elizabeth. "In a minute."

Enid breezed out of the cottage. When she was alone, Elizabeth looked down again at the *Manford House* help-wanted ad. What Enid said made sense . . . on the surface. *"It's wonderful that Mrs. Mueller takes these homeless kids under her wing . . . she just loves to help people. . . ."*

Yes, on the surface it sounded reasonable and even admirable. But Elizabeth's gut instinct told her that Mrs. Mueller's motive for employing only runaway kids, young people without homes or families or education to fall back on, was less than philanthropic. *And then there's Katya . . . Mrs. Mueller didn't do too good a job taking care of her,* Elizabeth reflected.

Enid thought Elizabeth was being paranoid and suspicious, but Elizabeth knew she had good cause. There was definitely something fishy going on at Paradise Spa—something that may have cost an innocent young girl her life—and Elizabeth was determined to get to the bottom of it.

Elizabeth knocked lightly on Mrs. Mueller's office door, which was slightly ajar. "Come in, my dear, come in," Mrs. Mueller called, beckoning with a smile.

Elizabeth stepped into the office but didn't take the chair that Mrs. Mueller waved to. "I can tell you're busy—I won't take up much of your time," Elizabeth said, eyeing the stack of papers on Mrs. Mueller's desk. "I just wondered if you knew anything about the autopsy, if they found out how Katya died."

"Autopsy?" Mrs. Mueller frowned. "There will be no autopsy. Circumstances don't warrant one—there is no question as to the cause of death."

Elizabeth was thrown off balance by the older

woman's vehemence. "Oh. I just thought . . . well, it seemed to me that there definitely *might* be a question, when someone as young and healthy as Katya—"

"She had a heart condition," interrupted Mrs. Mueller, her flat tone discouraging further discussion. "It is a tragedy, especially as we are unable to contact her family—she never provided the spa with any information about next of kin." Mrs. Mueller paused; with a visible effort she smiled at Elizabeth. "Now, my dear, if you'll excuse me. As you observed, I *am* rather busy. . . ."

"Sure," said Elizabeth. "Well . . . thanks."

Backing into the hall, she closed the door to Mrs. Mueller's office behind her. She'd intended to ask Mrs. Mueller about the spa's help-wanted advertisements in publications like *Manford House,* but now she was glad she hadn't had the opportunity. *I'll sleuth around a little bit more on my own,* Elizabeth decided. *I don't trust Mrs. Mueller. I don't trust her one bit.*

Jessica and Lila reclined side by side at the pool, their eyes closed and faces tipped to the sun. "I'm starting to get bored," Lila announced out of the blue.

"Bored?" Jessica repeated in disbelief. "How on earth can you be bored? We're at Paradise Spa, where there's something different to do every hour of the day. We haven't had a dull minute since we got here!" She ticked off the highlights on her fingers. "I met Alex, I found Katya's body in the steam room—"

She shivered at the memory.

"Well, what about *me*?" said Lila, somewhat plaintively. "*I* haven't met anybody. Sure, I've had facials and manicures galore, and I've busted my buns jogging and doing aerobics, but I'm telling ya, that stuff's starting to lose its novelty. I'm almost looking forward to going back to Sweet Valley. I mean, at least there we can go shopping and watch TV and—"

Jessica had sat up in her chaise lounge to smooth some more suntan lotion on her bronzed arms and legs. Now she interrupted Lila's lament by giving her friend's chair a swift kick. "Good-bye, boredom!" Jessica hissed. "There he is, and if you don't go up and talk to him this time, I'm totally giving up on you!"

At Jessica's announcement Lila sat bolt upright. Sure enough, her mystery man had just entered the pool area, a towel draped over one muscular shoulder and a paperback book tucked under his arm.

Lila sprang up from her chair. "This is it," she told Jessica. "This is really it. D day!"

With that she discreetly adjusted her skimpy coral-pink bikini, grabbed her towel and fashion magazine, and stormed across the redwood deck. She reached her mystery man before he could sit down . . . or see her coming and run.

After all the time she'd spent chasing him, there didn't seem any point in being roundabout. "Hi, I'm Lila," she said, gesturing to the chair next to his. "Is this taken?"

"Nope, it's all yours," he replied with a heart-stopping smile.

It's all yours . . . the words Lila wanted to hear, the chance she'd been dying for to get to know him. Something about the moment wasn't quite right, however.

"Excuse me, what did you say?" she asked.

"I said it's all yours," he repeated. He took off his sunglasses, revealing eyes even more sexy and beautiful than she'd dreamed. "Have a seat. Oh, and by the way, I'm Michael."

Lila gaped at him. *It can't be,* she thought, crushed. That squeaky, Mickey Mouse voice—it simply couldn't belong to that face, that body! It just wasn't fair!

But the voice was inescapable. "I've noticed you around," Michael told Lila. Each high-pitched syllable grated on her nerves like fingernails on a chalkboard. "Are you enjoying the spa?"

"Uh, yeah," Lila said, suddenly desperate to find a way out of the conversation. "Um, how about you?"

"It's a fantastic break," declared Michael with enthusiasm. "Just getting away from the whole Hollywood scene . . ." He paused in a self-important fashion, letting her digest this for a moment, then continued. "I work at a film-production company. Casting."

Ordinarily, Lila would have been in a swoon over all this. It was a not-so-secret fantasy of hers that someday she'd be "discovered" and whisked off to star in a blockbuster movie opposite a sexy matinee idol. Now her big chance had landed right in her lap!

And she couldn't wait to get away from the guy. "Well, don't get too much sun," Lila blurted out. "I just realized I'm late for a body wrap. Catch you later!"

Lila practically sprinted back around the pool. She grabbed Jessica's arm, yanking her out of the chair. "Come on, we're getting out of here."

Jessica gaped at her. "Back so soon? What happened? Don't tell me he blew you off, the jerk—"

"He didn't blow me off. Come on, hurry! In case he comes after me!"

Jessica was completely befuddled. "What did he do, make a pass at you or something?"

"No, he was perfectly friendly and nice," said Lila, striding away from the pool area and hauling Jessica with her. "Perfectly polite. He's a casting agent from Hollywood."

"What?" Jessica slammed on the brakes. "Lila, what is your problem? This guy sounds like a dream come true!"

Lila shook her head. "Take my word for it, he's not."

"How could you even tell from a conversation that lasted all of thirty seconds?"

"Believe me, I could tell," said Lila.

"So what was his fatal flaw?" asked Jessica. "Dirty fingernails? Halitosis? Cheap cologne?"

"Worse," promised Lila. "It was his voice."

"His voice," repeated Jessica.

Lila nodded. "He talked"—she raised her own voice to a ridiculous falsetto—"like this."

Jessica giggled. "You're kidding. Really?"

"He sounded like he'd just taken a big mouthful of helium."

"And you couldn't live with an itty-bitty drawback like that, with all the other things that guy has going for him?"

Lila shook her head emphatically. "He opened his mouth, and it was like someone dumped a bucket of cold water over my head. The biggest turnoff I've ever experienced!"

Jessica was doubled over with laughter. "Oh, God. I can't wait to tell this story to Alex."

"Yeah, ha ha," said Lila humorlessly. "Ha ha ha. Come on. Since we're stuck at this dumb spa till Saturday"—she grimaced—"let's go *aerobicize.*"

Late in the afternoon the twins, Lila, and their mothers gathered with a few other Paradise Spa guests and staff members on the lawn outside the fitness center, where they'd met Katya a few mornings earlier for the run to the waterfall. It had been

Elizabeth's idea to return to the waterfall in remembrance of Katya, and when she'd broached the subject to Mrs. Mueller, the older woman had encouraged it. "I can't think of a better way to honor her spirit," Elizabeth said now, choking back a tear.

They started off. Elizabeth fell in step alongside Lulu and Terry, another waitress. "I'm so sad about Katya," Elizabeth confided to the other two girls. "I keep thinking about her family, wherever they are, and it breaks my heart. They don't even know she's dead—they may *never* know!"

Lulu sighed. "She ran away from home, after all—maybe they wouldn't care."

Elizabeth thought about the framed picture standing on Katya's otherwise bare desk, and the way Katya had spoken about her mother. "I think they *would* care," she said softly.

They continued walking through the forest. Elizabeth glanced at Lulu and Terry. There was a question she very much wanted to ask them, but she didn't want to alienate them by being too blunt. "I guess Katya was lucky to find her way to Paradise Spa," began Elizabeth. "She had a good job here, and a nice surrogate family. Did you know she answered a help-wanted ad in a magazine she read at a shelter for runaways?"

Lulu nodded. "We talked about it, because that's how I got my job, too."

Elizabeth's heart skipped a beat. "You ran away from home, Lulu?"

"Yes, and so did Terry. Didn't you, Ter?"

Terry confirmed this. "Living in the shelter was awful," she recalled. "When I first came to Paradise Spa, I thought I'd died and gone to heaven."

Elizabeth was thrilled at this confirmation of her theory about the Paradise Spa employees, even though she didn't yet know what it all signified. "How long have you been working here?"

Lulu had been at Paradise for two years, and Terry for just under one. "And you're happy here?" asked Elizabeth. "You don't want to go back home?"

Lulu looked at her blankly. "Why would I want to go home?" she responded. "My parents were horrible to me, incredibly mean—that's why I left. And it's wonderful here."

"It really is," agreed Terry. "I wouldn't go back to Pennsylvania, even if I had the money."

"So you've thought about it," pressed Elizabeth. "You just haven't been able to save enough yet?"

Terry glanced at Lulu and they both laughed. "It's kind of hard to save money when you don't make any," Terry commented.

Elizabeth was puzzled. "What do you mean? Doesn't Mrs. Mueller pay you very well?"

Terry laughed again. "She doesn't pay us at all. Didn't you know that?"

Elizabeth was flabbergasted. "You mean, you work for *free*?"

"For room and board," Lulu corrected. "It's a great deal, really. When you think of what Mrs. Mueller saved us from . . ." She shuddered. "Life on the streets for a runaway is a nightmare."

"Still, to work for no salary!" Elizabeth exclaimed. "Don't you feel you're being exploited?"

Both girls shook their heads in an emphatic no. "We have companionship, beautiful surroundings, we're gaining valuable work experience, and Mrs. Mueller mentors and mothers us," said Lulu. "What more could we ask?"

"But if you want to go someplace . . ." Elizabeth remembered that the staff wasn't allowed to leave the grounds, even on their days off. "If you decide to leave the spa for good, go work somewhere else . . ."

"I can't imagine that happening," Terry said simply.

"I'm here to stay," agreed Lulu.

Elizabeth stared at the two girls, and they looked back at her with bland, impenetrable smiles. They sounded sincere . . . but they also sounded a little bit programmed. *Like they've practiced this speech,* Elizabeth thought. *Like they've given it many times before . . . or had it given to them.*

Despite the girls' protestations of satisfaction, the more she thought about it, the more the whole situation struck Elizabeth as extremely odd. She remembered all the times she and Jessica had got upset about one thing or another when they were growing up, and considered running away. *It was always to get Mom's and Dad's attention,* Elizabeth reflected, *not because we actually wanted to leave home for the rest of our lives.* Were the young people who worked at Paradise Spa really so different? Didn't they ever change their minds?

Enid relaxed in the chair in Mrs. Mueller's office. She didn't mind missing the memorial hike up to the waterfall with the others; she'd much rather sit and talk with Mrs. Mueller. *I feel so comfortable here,* she thought, glancing around the office, *so at home. I can tell Mrs. Mueller anything, and she always knows just what to say to make me feel better.*

"I can't believe in a few days I have to go home again," Enid remarked.

Mrs. Mueller gazed at Enid. "You're not looking forward to it, are you?"

Enid shook her head. "No."

"Because you're not happy at home, and lately you've felt like an outsider at school, too."

"Things will probably get better," Enid said without much conviction. "Sometimes it's just rotten being sixteen!"

"Yes, I remember." Mrs. Mueller sighed deeply. "I remember all too well how awkward the teenaged years can be, when one's feelings are so sensitive, so easily bruised." A spasm of pain distorted her face. "Damage done in those years can last a lifetime. . . ." Her expression cleared; she smiled benevolently. "I *do* understand, my dear, what you are going through."

"I know you do," said Enid, her eyes sparkling with grateful tears. "You've been so kind."

"It's because you remind me of my younger self, and when I look at you, I see . . . a second chance." Mrs. Mueller leaned close to Enid, her eyes glittering. "I'd like to spare you the pain and humiliation I suffered in life," she said in hushed, portentous tones. "I can do that for you, Enid. I can make your life perfect—I can make *you* perfect."

Enid gazed at Mrs. Mueller, her face open and trusting. Hope flooded her veins like an intoxicant; belief filled her heart. *She can do it,* Enid thought. *She's promised me, and I know she won't disappoint me. All I have to do is give her my answer: yes or no. . . .*

Enid was ready to take the plunge—ready to sever her ties to her old self, her old life. "OK," she told Mrs. Mueller, her voice clear and firm. "I'm ready."

Elizabeth and the others reached the crest of the hill deep in the forest. They heard the splash of the waterfall and smelled the mossy freshness of the natural pool where they'd cooled off after their run with Katya. "I feel close to Katya here," Elizabeth whispered to her mother.

Alice nodded. "Me, too."

While the rest of the group removed sneakers, shorts, and T-shirts in preparation for a swim, Elizabeth and Jessica sat down in the sun on the large, flat rock. "I'm going to bake for a few minutes before getting wet," said Jessica.

"Good idea," her sister agreed.

Having stripped down to her one-piece maillot, Jessica lay back on the rock. "Too bad the boys couldn't come," she commented. "Alex was working. How about Chris?"

Elizabeth clasped her arms around her knees. "He's working, too. But I saw him this morning. Wait'll you hear this!"

Elizabeth recounted her conversation with Chris and then told her sister about finding the page from *Manford House* in Katya's room. Jessica sat up to stare at Elizabeth, suitably impressed. "Wow. Alex is a runaway? I had no idea!"

"I guess he doesn't like to talk about it. Chris doesn't, anyhow."

Jessica tilted her head to one side. "You know, maybe that explains it."

"Explains what?"

"This weird feeling I got when I was with him last night, these strange vibes," said Jessica. "I like him a lot—he's gorgeous and sexy and fun—but sometimes he seems a little . . . I don't know. A little *off*."

Elizabeth nodded; she'd had the same experience with Chris. "I know *exactly* what you mean."

"But that must be it," said Jessica, looking pleased at having figured it out. "He's a runaway, and maybe he wasn't planning to tell me that, and so he had this secret that he was hiding and it made him a little uncomfortable." She lay back down. "Boy, what a relief. I was starting to think there was something wrong with him!"

"But there *is* something wrong," said Elizabeth. "Don't you think this is pretty suspicious, Jess? Mrs. Mueller hiring all these runaway kids? And Katya was so unhappy, and then she got yelled at for taking us near that white building, and now she's dead. Mrs. Mueller told the hospital Katya had a heart condition, so there's not going to be an autopsy. I think *she's* hiding something, don't you?"

Jessica snorted. "Liz, you should write for one of those mystery shows on TV—your imagination is totally over the top. Are you actually telling me you think Mrs. Mueller *murdered* Katya?"

"I'm saying I think *someone* murdered Katya, and Mrs. Mueller knows who and why," declared Elizabeth.

Jessica laughed out loud. "That is the most ridiculous thing I've ever heard in my entire life. Sweet old Mrs. Mueller . . . ?"

"She's not so sweet, and she's not so old," insisted Elizabeth. "She's Mom's age!"

"OK," conceded Jessica, for the purpose of argument. "So what's her motive for killing Katya, and how did she do it without leaving any marks? And what does Katya's death have to do with the fact that most, if not all, of the staff are runaways—who, by the way, with the exception of Katya, all really like Mrs. Mueller and seem incredibly happy at the spa? How does it all hang together?"

Elizabeth bit her lip. "I don't know. I haven't put all the puzzle pieces together."

"Because they're *not* puzzle pieces," said Jessica. "They don't add up to anything, except maybe to prove that you're a nutcase!"

Elizabeth sighed, discouraged. Jessica was right about one thing, anyway. "They don't add up to anything," she admitted. "Yet."

Her sister made a humphing noise. Ignoring her, Elizabeth gazed out at the waterfall, her chin resting on her tucked-up knees. Her mother and Mrs. Fowler were sitting at the edge of the pool chatting; Lulu, Terry, and Lila were having a playful water fight with Randall and Chelsea Spencer.

Elizabeth watched her mother rise to her feet and walk carefully along the rocks that bordered the pool. Alice neared the waterfall and put out a hand to test the spray. Elizabeth turned back to Jessica for a moment. "You know, there might be a motive for killing Katya," she said. "It could have something to do with that white building, the private, off-limits one. What if—"

She broke off her question when she heard Mrs. Fowler's voice rise above the sound of falling water. "Alice? Alice, where are you?"

Elizabeth turned her head. Just a few seconds before, her mother had been standing in front of the waterfall; now she was nowhere to be seen. Elizabeth jumped to her feet. "Mom!" she shouted.

Grace, too, continued to call out. "Alice. Alice!"

Now Jessica was on her feet. "What happened to Mom?" she asked Elizabeth.

Elizabeth shook her head. "I don't know. She was right over there a minute ago, and now she's . . ."

Together they ran over to Mrs. Fowler. "We were just talking, and now I can't find her anywhere," Grace said, her forehead creased with worry.

The others had climbed from the pool and were toweling themselves off. "No one saw her fall in, did they?" asked Jessica.

"No, definitely not," said Lila.

"Then she must have walked off into the woods," concluded Elizabeth. "Come on. Let's look for her!"

They fanned out into the trees, all calling Alice's name. But as the minutes ticked by, it became increasingly clear to Elizabeth that they weren't going to find her.

A needle of fear pierced Elizabeth's heart. The mysteries of Paradise Spa were multiplying. Her mother had disappeared without a trace!

Chapter 11

The twins raced back down the hill to Paradise Spa as fast as their legs would carry them, with the others following at an only slightly more moderate pace. Panic drove Elizabeth like a whip at her heels; she was panting with exertion, but she didn't even feel the burning in her lungs. All she could think about was her mother. *Something's happened to Mom. Something terrible's happened to Mom. . . .*

She and Jessica went straight to Mrs. Mueller's office. "Mrs. Mueller!" Jessica cried, pounding on the door. "Mrs. Mueller!"

They burst into the office without waiting for an invitation. Mrs. Mueller glanced up at them in surprise. "My dears, what on earth is the matter?" she exclaimed.

"Our mother. Up at the waterfall," Elizabeth gasped. "She disappeared!"

"What do you mean, disappeared? Now, sit down and tell me everything. *Slowly.*"

Obediently, Elizabeth and Jessica sank into chairs across the desk from Mrs. Mueller. "We walked up to the waterfall, a bunch of us," Jessica began, "in memory of Katya, because it was her favorite place."

Mrs. Mueller nodded. "Yes, I knew you were planning to do that."

"And we went for a swim in the natural pool below the waterfall," Elizabeth continued.

"Some of us did," said Jessica. "You and I didn't."

"Right, some of us." Elizabeth had caught her breath now; she spoke with more precision and care. "My mother was swimming, and then she was sitting on the rocks above the pool, and then she was standing in front of the waterfall, and then . . . she was gone."

"Gone." Mrs. Mueller held her hands together in a prayerful attitude, her chin resting on her fingertips. "You mean, she wandered off into the woods for a stroll?"

Elizabeth shook her head. "She wouldn't have done that without telling us where she was going."

"Ah, you never know. Perhaps she wanted to be alone," suggested Mrs. Mueller.

"But she would have heard us calling her!" said Jessica. "She would have known we were worried and come back."

"Perhaps by the time you realized she was missing, she was out of earshot," said Mrs. Mueller.

"Only a few seconds had passed," argued Elizabeth. "She couldn't have gotten far."

"And yet she—how did you express it?—'disappeared.'" Mrs. Mueller smiled tolerantly. "You are very precious to be so concerned about your beloved mother, my sweets. But I think the explanation is simple: She desired some time to herself. My guests often grow contemplative and seek adventure on their own. Paradise Spa is a perfectly safe environment for a 'solo'—there's no reason at all for you to worry. Your mother will return soon and be happy and refreshed as a result of her little walk in the woods."

Jessica looked somewhat less frantic after Mrs. Mueller's soothing speech, but Elizabeth was far from comforted. "It's just not like my mother to do something like that," she insisted. "I think we should form a search party and look for her."

Mrs. Mueller laughed lightly. "*I* think we should respect her wish for privacy. Let's give her an hour or two, shall we?"

Jessica nodded agreement. Elizabeth stared hard at Mrs. Mueller; Mrs. Mueller gazed back at her, unperturbed. "All right," Elizabeth said at last, grudgingly. "An hour. And then I'm going back up the hill to look for her, and if nobody else wants to help, that's fine."

She stalked out of the room, her heart pounding. Jessica trotted after her. "Do you really think something happened to her?" Jessica asked fretfully.

"I just don't know," said Elizabeth. Suddenly she had an idea. "Come on. Let's go back to the cottage and call Dad. He'll know what to do!"

They hurried back to the cottage. Lila and Mrs. Fowler were sitting in the living room. "Any sign of your mother?" Grace asked when the twins entered.

Elizabeth shook her head. "We're about to call my dad. He might have some advice."

Jessica picked up the phone. She listened for a moment, her forehead wrinkled. "No dial tone," she announced. "The line's dead!" She and Elizabeth stared at each other. "What are we going to do now?"

After a tense moment the group decided on a strategy. While Elizabeth looked around for a phone that worked, Jessica would tell Mrs. Mueller about the problem with the phone in their cottage; in the meantime Lila and her mother would search the grounds for Alice on the off chance that she'd returned to the spa and didn't realize everyone was worried about her.

"We'll reach Dad somehow," Elizabeth promised Jessica before they went their separate ways. "And we'll find Mom. And then"—her eyes clouded—"I wouldn't mind if we cut our trip short and went home early. I'm starting to think Paradise Spa is bad luck."

Jessica retraced their steps back to the main building and Mrs. Mueller's office. The door was closed; she lifted her hand to knock. Then she hesitated.

Mrs. Mueller was talking to someone. *She's on the phone,* Jessica realized with a rush of relief. *Great! That means I can call Dad from here.*

Not wanting to interrupt, she waited until she heard Mrs. Mueller hang up. Then she knocked loudly. "Mrs. Mueller? It's Jessica again. May I come in?"

"Of course, of course," Mrs. Mueller sang out.

Jessica hurried in. "The phone in our room isn't working, and I need to call my father," she announced. "May I use your phone, please?"

To her surprise Mrs. Mueller shook her head. "I'm afraid that's not possible. I've just discovered that all the phone lines at the spa are dead. I'm going to have to send one of the boys into town for a repairman."

"But—" Jessica bit back the rest of the sentence. *But I just heard you using the phone yourself. You're lying!* "Oh. That's too bad," she said. "Well . . . thanks anyway."

She retreated back into the hall, her mind whirling. Mrs. Mueller was lying, no doubt about it. But why? *Her phone is working and ours isn't—maybe they've been selectively disconnected?—but she wants me to think all the lines are down,* Jessica reflected. Again, why? To prevent Jessica and Elizabeth from contacting the outside world for help?

The possibility made Jessica's blood run cold as ice water. *Maybe Liz was right about Katya being murdered. Maybe there* is *something awful going on at Paradise Spa. And now Mom's missing. . . . Oh, God, what have they done with her?*

As she stood in the corridor chewing her fingernails, Jessica heard a noise from inside Mrs. Mueller's office. Hurried footsteps approached the door. There was a large potted palm at a bend in the hall, and Jessica quickly darted behind it for cover. She peered through the fronds, her heart galloping; Mrs. Mueller's door swung open.

Mrs. Mueller stepped out of the office, then locked the door behind her. Without glancing toward Jessica and the palm tree, she bustled down the hall in the opposite direction.

She's in a big rush, Jessica noted, emerging from her hiding place. *I wonder where she's going.*

She decided that wasn't important—as long as Mrs. Mueller was gone from the office for five minutes. That's all the time it would take to sneak in through a window and put through a phone call to her father at his office in Sweet Valley. . . .

Jessica left the building through a side door. After a quick check to make sure no one was watching, she ducked down and crawled through the shrubbery along the outside of the building until she was directly underneath Mrs. Mueller's office window.

The window was open. In thirty seconds Jessica had pushed it up and clambered over the sill. Rushing to the desk, she grabbed the telephone. The sound of a dial tone greeted her ear. "Hallelujah!" she exclaimed.

Rapidly, she punched in her father's office number. As she waited for him to answer, she scanned Mrs. Mueller's bookshelves. Something caught her eye just as her father's voice mail picked up. "You've reached the law office of Ned Wakefield. I'm with a client, but if you leave a message after the tone, I'll return your call as soon as possible. For further assistance press 'one' now."

The tone sounded. "Dad, it's me, Jessica," she said breathlessly. "I really need to talk to you—it's urgent. As soon as you can, please call the main desk at the spa and ask them to come find me or Liz. If you can't get through, if the line's out of order . . . call the police."

She hung up the phone. Her father was sure to panic when he heard her message, but that was OK. The best thing that could happen would be for him to hop into his car and drive straight up to Paradise.

The phone call completed, Jessica turned to the bookcase and the object that had caught her attention. Next to a row of textbooks about health and fitness, there was a tall, slim volume bound in deep-purple leather. "A Sweet Valley University yearbook, from the year Mom graduated!" she said out loud. "That's funny. Mom said she and Dad were both pretty sure they didn't know Mrs. Mueller back in college. Why would Mrs. Mueller have a yearbook from a school she didn't go to?"

Reaching up, Jessica lifted the yearbook from the shelf. It fell open in her hands to a dog-eared page. There was a rectangular hole in the middle of the page where a photo had been cut out.

As Jessica read the words beneath the blank space, an icy fist of fear tightened around her heart. "Alice Robertson, Most Popular Girl on Campus," read the caption.

Jessica stared at the hole where the photo had been, as chilled as if she were looking at a ghost. Why did Mrs. Mueller have Jessica's mother's old yearbook, and why had she cut out Alice's face?

After parting with Jessica, Elizabeth made a beeline for the pro shop. She found Chris adjusting the neatly folded piles of kelly-green Paradise Spa golf shirts on a display table.

"Chris, I need your help," she announced without preamble.

Chris looked up at her, taking in the tousled hair and wild eyes. "Liz, what's the matter?"

Rapidly, she spilled the story of her mother's

disappearance. "Your phone—I need to use your phone," she begged. "Is it working?"

"Uh . . ." Chris glanced over his shoulder at the telephone near the cash register. "No, actually I just noticed that it's not. I haven't had a chance yet to figure out what the problem is."

"Shoot, then I can't call Dad." She rubbed her eyes, thinking hard. "I just don't know what to do!" she cried desperately.

"Well . . ." Chris's manner remained irritatingly even and unruffled. "Have you talked to Mrs. Mueller? I'm sure she can help."

"She was no help at all. She just said not to worry—Mom is probably just walking in the woods and will wander back any minute now."

Chris lifted his shoulders. "So that's probably the case."

"But it's not," Elizabeth cried. "She's in trouble, I just know it. Will you come with me to look for her?"

Chris shifted on his feet uncomfortably. "I really can't leave the pro shop."

"But it's an emergency!"

He shook his head. "Without Mrs. Mueller's permission . . . I'm sorry, Liz."

"Mrs. Mueller's permission . . ." Elizabeth bit back the hot, angry words that sprang to her lips. "So you won't help me."

"It doesn't look like there's anything I can do. And I don't think you should go running around looking for her. Take my advice, Liz," Chris added, his eyes solemn. "Do what Mrs. Mueller says. Take it easy. Wait."

Elizabeth nodded, even though she had no intention of sitting around and waiting. "See ya," she said, masking her disappointment.

"You bet," he replied.

Disturbed by her unproductive conversation with Chris, Elizabeth trailed dejectedly back to Tranquillity Cottage. It was empty—Jessica, Lila, and Mrs. Fowler had yet to return from their respective errands, and there was still no sign of Enid. At a loss about what to do next, Elizabeth picked up the phone one more time. Silence met her ear instead of the familiar dial tone. Yep, it was out of order.

Then a second possibility occurred to her. Maybe the problem was the telephone itself rather than the phone line. *In which case I could E-mail Dad on my computer!* Elizabeth thought hopefully.

It seemed unlikely, given that the pro-shop phone wasn't working either, but it didn't hurt to check. Grasping the phone cord, she traced it behind the sofa to the jack. To her surprise, instead of being plugged into the wall, the cord came loose in her hand. Elizabeth stared down at it. The wire had been neatly severed in two. "Someone cut it!" she said out loud in disbelief. "Someone who didn't want us to make a phone call. . . ."

She didn't have time to think about what that might mean. Instead, hurrying into her bedroom, she carried her laptop computer over to the coffee table. Removing the dangling end of the useless phone cord from the jack, she plugged her computer into the line. It was working!

In a matter of seconds she'd logged on and sent an E-mail message to her father, requesting an immediate reply.

She waited impatiently. The minutes ticked by, but the computer screen remained blank. "C'mon, Dad," Elizabeth muttered. "Where are you? Would you check your E-mail, please?"

She sent another desperate message, to no avail. Apparently her father was away from the office, and she had no way of knowing when he'd return.

Elizabeth punched the sofa pillow in frustration. "I can't just sit here doing nothing," she declared, staring at her computer. "I wish *you* could talk to me. I wish *you* could help."

The computer looked silently back at her. Of course it couldn't talk, not in a human manner. But all at once Elizabeth remembered what Olivia had told her the other day. If Elizabeth dialed into her account at the *Oracle,* she could access INFOMAX and all the other services available to the computers on the school newspaper network. *INFOMAX can't tell me where Mom is,* Elizabeth thought as she typed rapidly, *but maybe it can answer some of my other questions. . . .*

Enid . . . Enid was someone else who was "missing," though in a different sense. What was going on with her lately? *She's really succumbed to the spa thing,* reflected Elizabeth. But it was more than that. From the start Mrs. Mueller had taken a special interest in Enid and exercised a special influence over her. The freckle treatments, the private counseling sessions, the diet, exercise, and vitamins . . . did they all add up to something?

On a hunch Elizabeth punched in her secret code and jumped on INFOMAX. Scanning the directory, she found a category called "Medicine and Health." Clicking on that, she studied the options for conducting research on-line.

One approach was to type in a list of elements, and the computer would tell her what they had in common. The example offered was a list of symptoms; the computer "diagnosed" the illness as the common cold. "Hmm," murmured Elizabeth. "I wonder what it will make of these 'symptoms'. . . ."

Quickly, she typed in everything she knew about the special therapies Enid had been undergoing at the spa at Mrs. Mueller's recommendation. She waited, breathless with suspense, as INFOMAX digested the data. Then a two-word answer appeared on the screen. It was so unexpected that Elizabeth felt the shock travel through her body like a lightning bolt.

The two words were: "Plastic Surgery."

Elizabeth clicked on "Continue," and a page of explanatory text filled the screen. She read it rapidly, her eyes widening. "Prior to the procedure the patient will undergo a series of conditioning treatments to prepare the body and skin for surgery. He or she will also take specially prescribed vitamins and restrict the diet under the guidance of the physician. In addition, the patient will be counseled by the physician regarding both the physical and emotional effects of plastic surgery. The physician will ascertain that the patient is making an informed decision before proceeding. . . ."

Elizabeth blinked, flabbergasted. She'd wondered what Enid's behavior meant, but this was simply preposterous. *Enid's getting ready to undergo plastic surgery? That's impossible!*

Just then the door to the cottage swung open. Mrs. Fowler and Lila rushed in. "Any luck?" Elizabeth asked eagerly.

Mrs. Fowler shook her head and sank into an armchair with a weary, discouraged sigh. "We looked absolutely everywhere," she related. "Every salon and fitness area, the steam room, the pools, the tennis courts, the golf course. We didn't find her, and no one has seen her recently."

"I'm really worried," said Elizabeth.

"Me, too," confessed Mrs. Fowler.

Elizabeth rubbed her forehead, thinking hard. "Something's going on at Paradise Spa, but I just can't figure out what it is," she exclaimed, frustrated. "OK, tell me what you think about all this."

Elizabeth ran over the strange events of recent

days. "First, there's Katya. Something was bothering her, and I think it wasn't just that she was lonely and homesick. Remember the white building, Lila? Katya wasn't supposed to take us near there, and Mrs. Mueller really chewed her out for it. Then, the night she was killed, I saw a note that fell out of Mrs. Mueller's pocket. Katya wanted to meet Mom—she was going to tell her something. But she was killed before she could."

"And now your mom's missing," said Lila. "God, you don't think . . ."

Elizabeth felt as if she were about to faint. Mrs. Fowler lifted a hand. "Let's not panic," she urged. "We won't be able to help Alice that way, if she is indeed in trouble. Liz, have you discovered anything else about Mrs. Mueller or Paradise Spa?"

"Only that practically everyone on the staff is a young runaway. Mrs. Mueller advertised in publications that were distributed at youth centers and shelters. It's weird," she said, shaking her head. "The kids all tell these terrible stories about their home life, and then they gush about how happy they are at Paradise, how Mrs. Mueller takes such good care of them and they never want to leave. Not only that, but they work for room and board—they don't even get salaries! And they can't leave the grounds, even on their days off."

"It's as if Mrs. Mueller casts some kind of spell over them," Grace remarked. "And Katya was the only one who didn't buy into it, or maybe she hadn't had time to adjust."

"A spell," repeated Elizabeth. "That's it, that's it exactly. Even Enid seems to be falling under it." She frowned, more worried than ever about both her mother and her friend. Finally the puzzle pieces seemed to be moving into place, and she didn't like the picture they made—not one bit. "It's as if Mrs. Mueller's brainwashed all her employees, making them believe they don't ever want to go home again," declared Elizabeth. "That way she can get them to work for practically nothing. And maybe she was afraid Mom found out her scheme!"

As the sun set, Mrs. Mueller's office grew dim, but Jessica didn't turn on a light for fear of being discovered. Having returned the Sweet Valley University yearbook to the shelf, she darted over to the door, unlocking it so she could make a speedy getaway if necessary. Then she turned to Mrs. Mueller's file cabinet.

One entire drawer was labeled "Staff." Anything might be a clue, Jessica thought, opening the drawer. *I might as well look through all of it.*

Inside, dozens of file folders were packed tightly together. Jessica read the labels with interest. "Katya, Lulu, Chris, Alex . . . there's one for each staff member!" she observed. "No, wait a minute." There were two files on each employee, one marked "Before" and the other "After." *Before and after what?* wondered Jessica, removing the Alex files.

Each of the folders contained a photograph. Moving over to the window, Jessica held them up to what remained of the light. "Oh, my God," she breathed.

The "After" photo was a picture of the boy Jessica knew: blond-haired, brown-eyed Alex of the perfect body and sculpted features. But the "Before" photo . . .

It was of an average-looking kid, also with brown eyes and somewhat darker hair. There was a resemblance to Alex, but only a subtle one. They had different noses, different cheekbones, even different chins.

Jessica shuffled the other pages contained in the "Before" file until she located a medical report. Suddenly it was clear beyond a shadow of a doubt. "Before" and "After" meant before and after radical plastic surgery!

Hurriedly, Jessica replaced the files about Alex and pulled the ones on Katya and Chris. Sure enough, they, too, contained "Before" and "After" pictures documenting dramatic changes in appearance. "Incredible," murmured Jessica, flipping through the rest of the files. "Everyone who works here has been completely made over. That explains why they're all so gorgeous!"

Then she saw a file with a name that didn't belong to a Paradise Spa employee. "Enid Rollins!" exclaimed Jessica.

It was a "Before" file; there was no "After"—yet. Opening the folder, Jessica slipped out two sheets. One was a photo of Enid, and the other a computer-generated image of another, more glamorous girl. A girl with hair similar to Enid's, but smoother and tawnier; a girl with Enid's green eyes, but a more elegant nose, fuller lips, a higher forehead. And her complexion . . . there wasn't a single freckle in sight!

"My God," Jessica whispered. "This is what Enid would look like . . . after plastic surgery!"

At that instant she heard a scraping sound behind her. The overhead light in the office snapped on.

Jessica whirled around with a startled gasp, the folder clutched in her hands and her back pressed against the wall. She was trapped.

Chapter 12

When she saw who was standing in the doorway, Jessica let out her breath in a gust of relief. "Boy, am I glad it's you!" she exclaimed. Her knees buckled and she dropped into a chair, fanning her flushed face with the folder. "I thought for sure it was Mrs. Mueller and I was in big trouble."

Enid closed the door behind her. "Why, what's the matter?" she asked. "What are you doing here?"

"I was just trying to make a phone call," explained Jessica, "a phone call that Mrs. Mueller didn't want me to make for some reason, and then I started snooping around a little. You'll never believe what I found out!" She waved the file at Enid, who was looking at her blankly. "Mrs. Mueller only hires people who've had plastic surgery—every single person on the staff at Paradise Spa has had a major overhaul. You should see the pictures, Enid. It's absolutely amazing, like Dr. Frankenstein or something—except instead of creating hideous monsters, Mrs. Mueller makes people gorgeous. And look!" For the coup de grâce, she whipped the computer-generated image from Enid's file. "She's even got a plan for *you*!"

Jessica expected Enid to be floored, speechless. Instead Enid smiled angelically. "I know. Isn't it wonderful?" she cooed, clasping her hands together. "I'm going to look the way I've always wanted . . . as beautiful as a supermodel!"

Enid took a few steps closer, and suddenly Jessica noticed a strange glaze in her eyes. *What's come over her?* she wondered. Jessica had always considered Enid Rollins the most boring person on the planet next to Elizabeth's boyfriend, Todd, and under any other circumstances she'd have encouraged Enid's spirit of adventure. But this was crazy.

"You can't be serious," Jessica said to Enid. "You're not going along with this—you're not actually considering plastic surgery!"

Enid continued to smile, but it was the frozen, mindless smile of a mannequin in a store window. "I've never been more serious about anything in my life."

"So what do we do now?" Lila asked her mother and Elizabeth.

The three were still sitting in the living room of Tranquillity Cottage.

"I say we confront Tatiana Mueller," voted Grace. "Go to her and demand to know Alice's whereabouts."

Elizabeth bit her nails nervously. "No," she said. "I mean, I want to find Mom, too, but I don't want to tip off Mrs. Mueller. I'm afraid of what she might do if she knows we're onto her. I mean, if she really did kidnap Mom or something."

"What's left, then?" asked Mrs. Fowler.

"We keep searching," replied Elizabeth.

"But we've already combed every inch of the spa," Lila reminded Elizabeth. "She's not here, Liz."

"No, she's not," Elizabeth had to agree. "But that only means she's somewhere else." She rose to her feet with sudden determination. "I'm going back up to the waterfall to look for her."

Mrs. Fowler glanced apprehensively at the window. "But it's getting dark!"

"I'll take a flashlight," said Elizabeth.

"Do you really think you'll find anything?" asked Lila.

Elizabeth shrugged. "It's the last place we saw her—if there's a clue anywhere, there may be one there. Besides"—having grabbed her flashlight, she was already halfway to the door—"I can't stand just sitting here doing nothing while the clock keeps ticking."

Alice stood up. "We'll come with you," she offered.

Elizabeth waved her back to her seat. "Someone needs to wait for Jessica. And in case anything happens to me . . ."

"Liz, be careful," Mrs. Fowler begged.

"I will," Elizabeth promised.

With that she hurried from the cottage and darted across the lawn toward the shadowy woods.

Leaving Enid standing in Mrs. Mueller's office, Jessica raced back to Tranquillity Cottage to tell Elizabeth what she'd learned. Instead of her sister, she found Lila and Grace. "Wait till you guys hear what's in Mrs. Mueller's file cabinet!" Jessica burst out.

As Lila and Grace listened in astonishment, Jessica described the "Before" and "After" photographs, and Enid's stunning admission that she was a candidate for plastic surgery. "Do you think this can possibly have anything to do with what happened to Katya, and the fact that Mom's missing?" she asked when she was finished with the story.

Mrs. Fowler's forehead creased in a puzzled frown. "Everything's getting more complicated by the minute," she remarked. "Liz thinks your mother may have found out about some plot to exploit runaway kids as a source of cheap labor. This plastic-surgery thing—I just don't—" A beeping noise interrupted her. "What was that?"

Jessica pointed to the laptop, still resting on the coffee table. "Liz's computer," she answered.

"It makes that noise when she gets a message. When she gets a message!" Jessica repeated, her eyes lighting up. "Hey, I bet Elizabeth was trying to E-mail Dad!"

All three of them crowded around the computer to read the return message that had flashed up on the screen. Sure enough, it was from Ned Wakefield.

Jessica read it aloud. "'Liz, I'm away from the office, but I just logged on to my portable and got your E-mail note. It sounded quite mysterious. Is something wrong?

"'Write back and let me know what's up. And in the meantime, would you do me a favor? Tell your mother she'll never believe this, but I've finally remembered who Tatiana Mueller is. We *did* go to college with her—she lived down the hall from your mom in the dorm junior year. Everyone called her Tatty Mule because she was so homely and pathetic. She worshiped your mother, though, and followed her around like a puppy dog. I didn't realize she was in the spa business—last I heard, she'd gone to medical school. That's all, kiddo. Get in touch.'"

"Medical school!" squeaked Lila. "Do you think that means Mrs. Mueller operated on the employees herself?"

"Tatty Mule . . ." Jessica's eyes were wide. "Ohmigod, now I understand. The yearbook!"

Lila and Grace stared at her without comprehension. Quickly, Jessica explained. "Mrs. Mueller has a Sweet Valley University yearbook on the bookshelf in her office from the year Mom graduated. I looked inside, and she'd cut out Mom's picture! That must be why—she worshiped Mom back in the old days."

"But why wouldn't she have said something to her?" wondered Grace. "Alice told me that she asked Tatiana if they'd been acquainted at any point in the past, and Tatiana distinctly said no."

Lila hugged herself, shivering. "Ugh, this is too creepy! It's just like this TV movie I saw once where this woman was obsessed with another woman and wanted to look just like her. She started dressing like her, wearing her hair the same way, hanging around her house and kids, calling her husband at the office pretending to be her . . ."

"But Mrs. Mueller's a doctor," Grace pointed out. "A plastic surgeon, from the sound of it."

"So she could do more than just pretend," said Lila, her eyes wide.

Jessica gaped at them. Suddenly everything fell into place. What would have seemed insane a few minutes before now seemed horrifyingly plausible. "Mrs. Mueller wants to trade places with Mom—she wants to trade *faces* with Mom!" Jessica cried. "Mom's in real danger. We have to find her, fast!"

"Elizabeth's looking for her right now," said Lila. "She went back up . . ."

Her sentence trailed off into nothing. All three

stared at one another, instantly thinking the same thing. "To the waterfall?" asked Jessica. Mrs. Fowler and Lila nodded. "Then Liz is in danger, too," declared Jessica. "Come on, there's not a minute to lose!"

Alice's lashes fluttered. With a supreme effort she managed to open her eyes a crack, even though her lids felt as if they were weighted down with stones. *Where am I?* she wondered groggily.

She could distinguish little about the room where she lay. It was dimly lit. The surface of the blank walls looked cobbled, uneven—were they made of stone, or was her blurry vision playing tricks on her?

She tried to move her arms and legs, to no avail. Like her eyelids, her limbs felt impossibly heavy. She struggled to understand the situation in which she found herself. *What happened to me? Was I attacked—have I been drugged? I'm lying on some kind of bed. Is this a hospital? Am I strapped down, or just too weak to move?*

She was alone in the strange room, but she had to get help somehow. If she called, someone was sure to come to her aid.

Alice tried to part her lips; she tried to move her tongue. Her throat tightened painfully, but she could emit no sound.

I'll rest, she thought, dizzy and discouraged. *I'll save my strength, and then in a few minutes I'll try again.*

Her eyelashes fluttered again; she felt herself sinking back into oblivion. Then she heard something, a movement nearby. Though her other senses were muted, her hearing was sharp. She heard the muffled sound of a footstep, of breathing. Someone had entered the room!

Again she tried unsuccessfully to speak. She opened her eyes as wide as she could to see the face of her savior.

A woman bent over her. Slowly, the vaguely familiar features swam into focus. *I know her,* Alice thought. Then, *No, it can't be. She was younger, and though she was plain, her face wasn't scarred, twisted. . . .*

Dressed as always in her white lab coat, Mrs. Mueller—Dr. Mueller—gazed down at Alice Wakefield. "So, Alice Robertson," she whispered with an eerie smile, "at last." She stroked Alice's cheek, lovingly, possessively. "For so many years I've dreamed of this face, coveted it. And soon . . ." She reached up to touch her own withered cheek, and her smile broadened. "Soon it will be my own!"

Suddenly Alice remembered where she'd met Tatiana Mueller. But before she could muster the resources to speak or struggle, another shadowy figure entered the room. As the sickly sweet scent of anesthetic filled the air, a mask was clapped firmly over Alice's mouth. Her vision blurred and darkened and she lost consciousness.

* * *

Elizabeth stumbled along the path up the hill. Above the trees the sky was a faint twilight pink, but in the woods it was already pitch-black. The small flashlight she carried offered little illumination; she continually tripped over exposed tree roots. When a bird darted suddenly overhead with a ghostly screech, Elizabeth let out a frightened yelp.

She stood for a moment, listening to the dusk. There were the occasional chirps of birds, the rustle of the wind in the leaves, and other mysterious woodland sounds. Elizabeth shivered. *I should have made Chris come with me whether he wanted to or not,* she thought, glancing around her apprehensively. *What if someone's following me?*

She started walking again, faster now, heedless of the branches that whipped her face. At a fork in the path she stopped for a moment, uncertain, and then continued to the right. She could now hear the music of falling water; she was almost there.

Ahead, there was a break in the gloom. Near the top of the hill a small clearing held back the trees, revealing a wedge of sky. Just beyond the clearing, Elizabeth remembered, was the base of the waterfall and the natural swimming pool.

She approached cautiously, fearfully, half expecting someone—her mother? who?—to step out from among the trees and accost her. But the night was still, almost peaceful. *You're the only one here,* Elizabeth told herself. *You have to do this, for Mom.* Mustering her courage, she pressed forward.

The pool lay before her, a sheet of silver shimmering in the twilight. Elizabeth clambered onto the rock where she and Jessica had sunbathed earlier that afternoon. *We were sitting right here when we saw Mom for the last time,* Elizabeth recalled, reconstructing the order of events, *and Mom and Mrs. Fowler were over there, and Lulu, Terry, Lila, Chelsea, and Randall were over there. . . .*

Carefully, she began to walk along the flat rocks that circled the pool. They were mossy and damp; at one point her foot slipped, and she came perilously close to plunging into the water. She continued a few more feet and then stopped.

"This is where Mom and Mrs. Fowler were sitting when they got out after their swim," Elizabeth said aloud, softly. "And then Mom walked toward the waterfall, like this. . . ."

Elizabeth retraced her mother's footsteps. Now the pool was to her right and the waterfall to her left; she could feel the cold, damp spray on her skin. "And the last I looked at her, Mom was standing here, her hand stretched out to test the water like this. . . ."

Again, imitating her mother's gesture, Elizabeth extended her fingers toward the waterfall. She had to brace her wrist against the pressure of the plunging stream. And then she felt something else. Something brushed against her bare ankle, then closed around it with a viselike grip. Screaming for help, Elizabeth tried to yank her leg free. Her struggle was futile. Relentlessly, the force dragged her toward the waterfall . . . *into* the waterfall!

Elizabeth was surrounded by rushing water, instantly drenched. When she tried to scream, her mouth and lungs filled with icy water. *I'm drowning,* Elizabeth realized, and she had only enough time to wonder . . . Had coming to the waterfall been the biggest—and last—mistake of her life?

Chapter 13

Suddenly Elizabeth could breathe again. The deafening rush of falling water had muted somewhat—it was no longer pounding right in her eardrums—and the feeling of being in the middle of a deluge had ceased. For a moment she stood doubled over, coughing and gasping. Then she straightened up and dashed the water from her eyes.

She looked around to see where she was. Damp, rocky outcroppings surrounded her; on one side was a wall of falling water. *It's a cave, an underground cave!* she thought. *I'm* behind *the waterfall! But how did I . . .*

Then she jumped. Someone was standing only a few feet away from her. Chris!

Elizabeth had never been so glad to see anyone in her entire life. "Chris!" she cried. "Where did you come from? And what happened to us—what is this place?"

She was about to fling herself into his arms, when she realized he was looking at her strangely. He stood with his arms folded across his chest; instead of being warm with concern and affection, his eyes were as cold as the stone walls of the cave.

Elizabeth froze in her tracks. "Chris?" she repeated, her voice trembling with uncertainty.

He took a step toward her. Now she noticed something else. Instead of his usual casual sports attire, he was wearing a clinical-looking white lab coat. In fact, he was dressed exactly like . . .

Mrs. Mueller.

She'd been wrong about Chris all along. He wasn't her friend—he wasn't there to save her life. He was the one who'd pulled her through the waterfall. He was one of Mrs. Mueller's henchmen!

The color drained from Elizabeth's face. She turned to run, but there was no place to hide.

Chris seized her arm in a fierce, unbreakable grip. "Let me go," Elizabeth pleaded.

Chris looked at her without emotion or compassion. "You're coming with me," he commanded, dragging her roughly toward a dark tunnel opening on the far side of the cave. His next words made Elizabeth's heart sink. "Mrs. Mueller is expecting you."

Jessica, Lila, and Mrs. Fowler scrambled around the cottage, searching for sturdy shoes, jackets, and flashlights. Jessica was close to panic. "Something terrible must have happened to Mom at the waterfall," she said, choking back a sob. "What if Liz . . . what if they both . . . what if we're too late?"

Finally they were ready to head out into the night. Before they even reached the cottage door, however, it swung open and Enid entered.

She took in their frantic, hurried appearance without blinking. "Where are you going?" she asked calmly, as if perhaps she thought they were heading to the salon for cucumber facials.

"Enid, you know something about all this," cried Jessica. "What's going on? Where are Mom and Liz? What has Mrs. Mueller done with them?"

Enid's expression remained bland and unconcerned. "Mrs. Mueller hasn't done anything wrong. There's absolutely nothing to worry about, Jessica," she said, her voice a spiritless monotone. "You shouldn't get so upset. I'm sure Liz and your mother are fine. Everything's fine, everything's—"

Racing over to Enid, Jessica grabbed her by the shoulders and started shaking her. "Everything's *not* fine, and you know it!" Jessica yelled in Enid's face. "This isn't a game, Enid. You have to help us!"

She continued to shake Enid with all her might. Enid had undergone some mysterious, horrible transformation, but Jessica was certain the real Enid, the old Enid, was still somewhere deep inside this strange new person who walked and talked as if in a daze. "Enid," said Jessica, her voice dropping to a desperate whisper, "Liz is in *danger*. Her *life* may be at stake."

Something flickered behind Enid's eyes—a faint glimmer of recognition. *She's coming back to us!* Jessica thought.

Then the light faded. Enid remained mute, staring at Jessica in stubborn silence.

Jessica turned away, feeling betrayed. "Forget it," she said to Lila and Mrs. Fowler. "Let's just go up to the waterfall. Maybe we'll catch up with her on the way. Maybe—"

"No," someone whispered.

Jessica whirled. The word had come from behind her.

Enid spoke again. "No," she said, her voice still small and faint, as if it were coming from a distance. "The waterfall . . . it's no use. They're at the clinic."

"The clinic?" repeated Jessica, confused.

"The white building," said Enid.

Chris strode briskly down the dank, shadowy tunnel, never relaxing his iron grip on Elizabeth's wrist. She trotted after him, stumbling over rocks and fighting back frightened sobs. "Chris, where are we going?" she asked repeatedly. "What's going on? Do you know where my mother is?"

But he seemed deaf to the pleading note in her voice. He didn't once look back at her or offer a single word of explanation or comfort.

The tunnel, lit only by faint, flickering lamps, twisted and branched as it gradually grew narrower. They took turn after turn, heading downward, deeper into the earth, and Elizabeth felt dizzy with claustrophobia. *It's like a tomb,* she thought, shuddering. *It's like being buried alive.*

But then, after a sharp turn into yet another tunnel, they started to climb again. Ahead, the light grew brighter. Elizabeth caught her breath, and all of a sudden something like hope blossomed inside her. *Maybe he's leading me to Mom. Please let her be alive,* she prayed silently. *Please let her be OK.*

The tunnel took one final turn, and Elizabeth and Chris found themselves face-to-face with a heavy iron door. As Elizabeth watched, Chris lifted his hand to a small keyboard panel next to the door and rapidly typed in some kind of password. With a deep whooshing sound the door slid open.

Elizabeth shielded her eyes. After the dimness of the cave and tunnels, the sudden brightness was blinding. Ahead stretched a long corridor painted a stark, sterile white; doors opened off the hall, but there were no windows.

This time Elizabeth didn't need to ask. She knew where she was. As Chris propelled her through the doorway, she exclaimed, "The white building!"

While Grace hurried to Mrs. Mueller's office to phone the police, Jessica, Lila, and Enid dashed off into the forest. The night was now black, and the footing treacherous; they were forced to walk slowly just to make sure they stayed on the path.

"We'll never get there in time!" Jessica fretted.

"Yeah, but if we get lost, we'll never get there at all," pointed out Lila.

Enid remained silent.

The biggest challenge was retracing the route they'd taken with Katya on the sunny afternoon a few days earlier. "I think this is where we started our Frisbee golf game," said Jessica, swinging her flashlight in an arc. "Remember that big rock?"

"Yes, and there's the stream and the tree stump," confirmed Lila.

"So we headed in this direction," decided Jessica, forging into the brush.

"No," Lila called after her. "I think we went that way."

Jessica stopped, looked at where Lila was pointing, and shook her head. "Uh-uh. I'm almost positive we headed directly away from the stream."

Both girls looked to Enid for a deciding vote. Then Jessica remembered. "That's right, you weren't there, were you?" she said. "And I bet you wouldn't help us out anyway." Enid had retreated once again into her shell; she stared at Jessica without comprehension, as if Jessica were speaking a foreign language.

Lila and Jessica faced each other stubbornly. "I really think I'm right," said Lila.

Jessica wavered. "Well . . ." She took another look around the densely wooded grove. It was all starting to look the same to her. "OK," she said at last. "We'll try your way."

Taking a deep breath, she forged ahead, keeping pace with Lila while Enid trailed behind them. The bushes and trees grew close together; they had to use their arms to fend off snapping branches. "I don't remember its being this overgrown," commented Jessica after a few minutes.

"That's because you were too busy making out with Alex to notice," said Lila, cursing under her breath as she dropped her flashlight.

"That's right. Alex!" Jessica hadn't thought about him all day. "Why didn't we get him to come with us? He'd know the way."

"Well, it's too late now," grumbled Lila. "Let's keep going. I think I see a clearing up ahead."

But if anything, the longer they walked, the wilder the forest grew. And scarier. "It's so dark, I can only see about three feet in front of my face," said Jessica. "Anything could be out there—a wild animal or . . ." She pictured Mrs. Mueller, wielding some kind of murderous surgical instrument, and her teeth started chattering. "What if we get attacked?"

Lila stopped abruptly in her tracks and clutched Jessica's arm. Jessica yelped. "What? What?"

"That tree—the one with the double trunk all wrapped in vines," said Lila. "Didn't we already pass it?"

"It must have been a tree that looks just like it," suggested Jessica.

Lila shook her head. "No, I'm sure of it. See that hanging bird's nest, the one that looks like a purse?" She pointed the flashlight. "I remember that. It's the same tree. And that means . . ."

She and Jessica stared at each other, their eyes wide with dread. "We've been going in circles," concluded Jessica, putting a hand to her sinking heart.

"We're lost," Lila confirmed miserably.

Chris marched Elizabeth down the long white corridor. At one point they passed a half-open door, and she caught a glimpse of what looked almost like a science lab. Two people in white lab coats—a young man and woman—were bent over some papers spread out on a counter.

Elizabeth wanted to take a second look, but Chris wouldn't tolerate lagging. Even without it, though, she was pretty sure she recognized both people. The girl was the beautiful blond Paradise Spa aerobics instructor, Candace, and the boy was . . . Jessica's Alex!

Jessica, thought Elizabeth. *Is she worried about me yet? Is she looking for me? Did she reach Dad—is he on his way? Or*—Elizabeth turned pale, imagining the worst-case scenario—*is she a prisoner of Mrs. Mueller, too?*

Chris stopped in front of an unmarked door at the end of the corridor, then knocked five times in quick succession. It sounded to Elizabeth like a code.

There was no audible reply, but the door slid silently open. *Remote control,* thought Elizabeth, holding her breath. Who—or what—was waiting for her on the other side?

The room was as white and bright and sterile as the rest of the building, or at least what Elizabeth had seen of it so far. It appeared to be an office: There were bookcases and file cabinets and a modern chrome desk. And seated at the desk . . .

Mrs. Mueller stood up as Elizabeth and Chris entered. Then she nodded briskly in dismissal at Chris.

He backed toward the door, preparing to leave Elizabeth alone with Mrs. Mueller. Elizabeth cast a last, pleading glance his way. *Help me,* she begged silently. *Don't go—don't abandon me.* But Chris wouldn't meet her eyes. He stepped back out into the hall, and the door slid shut again.

Elizabeth whirled to face Mrs. Mueller. She had no idea what Mrs. Mueller planned to do to her, but she knew she was better off not giving her a chance to do it. *I'm cornered—I'll have to bluff my way out of here,* she determined.

"I know all about what you're doing to these runaway kids," Elizabeth declared boldly.

Mrs. Mueller cocked her head to one side in that birdlike way of hers. "You do?" she said with an amused, quizzical smile.

"Yes. You entice them to Paradise Spa and then brainwash them into thinking they don't ever want to return home so they'll hang around permanently as cheap labor! And Katya resisted you, didn't she? She was about to blow your cover—she was going to tell my mother all about your racket. That's why you had to . . . do away with her."

Elizabeth expected Mrs. Mueller to puff up with outraged indignation and deny the accusation. Instead she chuckled indulgently. "Oh, my dear, I'm afraid you don't know the half of it." She waved toward the door, and it slid open as if by magic. "May I give you a tour of my facilities?"

Speechlessly, Elizabeth followed Mrs. Mueller into the corridor. The older woman carried a remote-control device; by pressing a button she was able to open any of the doors onto the hall. "Security is very tight here, as you can see," Mrs. Mueller informed Elizabeth. "Besides myself and Marguerite, only a limited number of trusted staff have access to this building. I observe my new employees for a lengthy time before deciding if they are fit to be trained as my special . . . assistants."

"Assistants to what?" asked Elizabeth.

Mrs. Mueller raised the remote control. A door slid open, revealing a room containing curtained-off beds, examining tables, and cabinets filled with gleaming medical instruments. "A doctor's office?" said Elizabeth, astonished.

"Yes. This is where we prepare the patients for surgery," said Mrs. Mueller.

Surgery . . . Elizabeth's heart skipped a beat as

she recalled what she'd learned from INFOMAX shortly before going in search of her missing mother. "Surgery . . . you mean *plastic* surgery. And you're the surgeon!" she guessed.

Mrs. Mueller nodded, looking pleased with Elizabeth's quickness. "That's right. Everything you see at Paradise Spa is my handiwork, right down to the exquisite faces of my employees."

Elizabeth was stunned. "You operated on *all* of them?"

"Each and every one, with Marguerite's help," Mrs. Mueller confirmed. "And they are works of art, no? Young gods and goddesses. Ah, what pleasure it gives me every day to look upon their lovely bodies and faces and know that I created them!"

Elizabeth was still struggling to comprehend. "But *why*?"

"Why?" Mrs. Mueller's homely brow furrowed. "Are you asking, Why beauty? Why not?" she countered. "Why would we want to be surrounded by anything else?"

"But the people who work here, the runaways—"

"Yes, the runaways. They have been a most gratifying source of material. It was Marguerite's idea, the clever girl. You see, we knew Marguerite would require many opportunities to practice the craft I was teaching her. . . . And the runaways—they are so eager to start life anew, to be made beautiful and worthy of love after a lifetime of neglect and rejection! A little gentle suggestion is all it takes in most cases."

A little gentle suggestion, in most cases . . . "Including Enid's?" demanded Elizabeth. "Have you been trying to alienate Enid from the rest of us and brainwash her into thinking she needs plastic surgery—is that what all the special vitamins and skin treatments and counseling sessions are about?"

Mrs. Mueller smiled. "And if it is? If it's what Enid desires?"

"But it's horrible!" Elizabeth declared. "You coerce those kids into having plastic surgery." She thought of another aspect of Enid's behavior—her negativity toward her mother. "And you make them hate their parents, don't you? Then after the operation it's not just that they don't *want* to go home again, but they *can't*—no one would recognize them. They've cut off all their options—they're trapped!"

"You talk as if I'm doing them a disservice," said Mrs. Mueller with a disapproving pout. "I make their fantasies come true! Think of it. The children come to Paradise escaping their troubled pasts. That in and of itself would be enough, but then, when they've settled in, with my guidance they are privileged to select the beautiful features they've always dreamed of possessing." Her voice grew intense, maniacal. "They are literally reborn," she hissed. "*I* do that for them. And most of them are grateful for the beauty I've bestowed on them, and the opportunities available to them at Paradise. Then there are a few like Katya. . . ."

Calm descended once more over Mrs. Mueller's distorted features, and she shrugged carelessly, as if murdering Katya was just a trivial part of doing business at Paradise Spa. *And it is, for her,* realized Elizabeth, her knees shaking like palm branches in the wind. *She's that ruthless. She's a madwoman! And I'm totally in her power. And so is . . .*

A terrible fear seized Elizabeth's heart. "What have you done to my mother?" she cried.

Chapter 14

Elizabeth's desperate question hung in the sterile air of the surgical prep room for a long, pregnant moment. But Mrs. Mueller didn't deign to answer it.

Instead she gave Elizabeth a preening, proprietary smile. "Come, let me show you the operating theater."

Elizabeth had no choice but to follow Mrs. Mueller across the room to another sliding door. It swished open.

What Elizabeth saw in the operating theater was even more terrifying than anything that had come before. In addition to an operating table and a bloodcurdling array of surgical equipment, there were pictures papering all four walls of the room. Huge blowup photographs, both color and black-and-white . . . of Alice Wakefield.

Elizabeth repeated her question, her voice trembling. "What have you done with my mother?"

Again Mrs. Mueller ignored her. "It's a lovely face, isn't it?" she said, waving a hand at the photographs. "Angelic, and yet also wholly human. The delicate features and coloring, the warm, feminine expression . . . this is the face *I* dream of. You know, I tried once before to look like your mother, when I was a young woman of twenty-three," she confided to Elizabeth. A bitter scowl twisted her face; she lifted a hand to her cheek. "But the surgeon was incompetent—he left me scarred, grotesque. But not forever!" Her voice rose triumphantly. "I refused to accept that fate. I spent the better part of the next two decades becoming the best plastic surgeon in the world so I could train someone I trust to transform me."

Elizabeth was fascinated by Mrs. Mueller's story even as she was repulsed and terrified. "Marguerite!" she guessed.

"Yes, Marguerite. And I succeeded," cackled Mrs. Mueller. "She is even better with the knife than I am. Remember Katya—lovely, foolish Katya? That face was Marguerite's masterpiece . . . until now."

"Now? Who—who is Marguerite going to operate on now?" stuttered Elizabeth.

"It's my turn," said Mrs. Mueller, her eyes gleaming. "At last, at long last . . ."

Elizabeth shot a glance at a smiling photograph of her mother—she recognized it as her mother's college-yearbook portrait—and then turned back to Mrs. Mueller, the hideous truth dawning. "The pictures. You mean—"

Mrs. Mueller nodded. "When the surgery is complete, I will be as much a twin to your mother as you are to Jessica."

Elizabeth staggered back a step, weak with horror. "No," she whispered.

"Yes," said Mrs. Mueller. "But the photographs weren't sufficient. Before we proceeded, we needed to see how Alice had aged—we needed to observe her in motion, in the living, breathing flesh. So I invited her to the spa." A shadow of regret dimmed the bright expectation in Mrs. Mueller's eyes. "And I've grown genuinely fond of her. I'm just sorry that there can't be two of us. . . ."

At that moment a door on the other side of the operating theater whisked open. Marguerite, dressed in mint-green surgical garb and mask, wheeled a gurney into the room. A patient was strapped onto it, unconscious and draped in a white sheet.

"Mom!" shrieked Elizabeth, lunging forward. "Get away from her. Let her go!"

Deep in the hilltop forest above Paradise Spa, Jessica sank down onto a fallen log and began weeping openly. "We'll never get out of here, and

Mom and Liz will die and it will be all my fault," she sobbed. "No, all *your* fault," she corrected herself, pointing an accusing finger at Lila. "You're the one who was so sure you knew the right way to the white building!"

"I'm doing my best," Lila snapped. "But you're right, we won't get out of here if you just give up and cry like a baby. C'mon." Grabbing Jessica's arm, she yanked her to her feet. "We don't have a minute to waste, remember?"

The three forged doggedly on. Suddenly Jessica noticed that the underbrush seemed thinner—she could actually see the dirt of the forest floor. "I think we're back on the path!" she shouted.

Sure enough, the going became easier. Next, Lila made a discovery. "Up there," she cried, shining her flashlight. "That thicket. Isn't this where you lost your Frisbee, and then when we ran around it, we saw the white building?"

Jessica hurried to find out. She sprinted toward the thicket at full speed, slapping branches out of her way. Then she was through the thicket and in the meadow on the other side . . . and there it was!

The white building glowed faintly in the night, like an alien spaceship. Jessica, Lila, and Enid ran toward it, arms pumping. "The door. Where's the door?" Jessica gasped breathlessly.

"Over there," said Lila. "But how will we get in? It's bound to be locked."

"You never know," said Jessica, her optimism

returning now that they were so close to their goal.

She reached the door first and pressed her body against it. "There's no knob or handle," she grunted. "Come on, help me push!"

They leaned all their weight against the door, to no avail. In desperation Jessica began pounding on it with her fists. It was too late for secrecy. "Let me in!" she hollered.

She was taken by surprise when the door slid open, and she stumbled into the building, nearly falling on her face. Lila and Enid followed close on her heels, but they were stopped short by the forbidding figures of two sturdy young men in white lab coats holding remote-control devices in their hands.

Alex and Chris frowned sternly at the three girls. "What are *you* doing here?" Alex barked at Jessica.

Jessica didn't need to ask what *they* were doing there. One look told her the boys weren't on her side . . . their souls belonged to the enemy. "Get ready to make a run for it," she hissed to Lila and Enid.

In a louder voice she said to the boys, "The operating room. Where is it?"

Without responding Alex stepped toward her, preparing to force her back out of the building. But Chris shot a nervous glance over his shoulder, inadvertently giving Jessica a crucial clue. "This way," she shouted to Lila and Enid. "Come on!"

She dashed past a startled Alex, elbowing him

hard in the side. The remote-control device flew from his hand, and Lila fielded it in midair.

The boys scrambled in hot pursuit, but the girls had gotten a head start, and they were running the race of their lives. "Down there, the last room on the left," Jessica panted to Lila, who lifted the remote control in readiness. "I just hope we're not too late!"

Elizabeth tried to run to her unconscious mother's side, but Mrs. Mueller restrained her, seizing her arm with clawlike fingers that were surprisingly strong. "There's nothing you can do for her," she told Elizabeth, her voice cruel and cold. "If you try to disrupt the proceedings, it will only hasten her inevitable end. Your mother's face can serve as a model for Marguerite during the surgery whether she is alive or dead. And as for you, my dear . . ."

Mrs. Mueller's grip on Elizabeth's arm became caressing; her evil smile was almost affectionate. "It's a pity, but now that you know the truth, well . . . the new Alice may have to be satisfied with only one loving and devoted daughter, named Jessica." In one swift motion Mrs. Mueller reached for a tray laden with shiny sterile instruments and seized a scalpel. "Yes, perhaps one of the precious twins will have a tragic accident"—she sketched the air in front of Elizabeth's face with the scalpel; Elizabeth cringed—"and disappear."

Elizabeth froze, her muscles tensed to run and her eyes glued to the deadly knife. One false move, and in an instant Mrs. Mueller would cut her throat. *And if I did escape, what about Mom?* Elizabeth asked herself.

There was only one option: She had to fight for her life.

Just as Elizabeth was about to spring on Mrs. Mueller, the door to the operating theater slid open. To Elizabeth's astonishment and delight Jessica, Lila, and Enid burst in. "Liz!" Jessica shrieked when she spotted her sister.

Thank God. We're saved! Elizabeth thought.

But immediately her hopes of liberation were dashed. Chris and Alex had been close on the heels of the three intruders, and now they stormed into the room as well. Within seconds Alex had grabbed Lila while Chris put an armlock on Jessica. Enid just stood, her back against the wall, her face pale and uncertain.

"Chris, call more security guards," Mrs. Mueller commanded, still threatening Elizabeth with the scalpel.

Chris began to drag Jessica across the room to a wall phone. Shifting his grip, he held her with one strong arm, then reached for the phone with the other.

Before he could lift the receiver, Elizabeth's voice rang out, clear and pure in the tense silence. "No!" she cried. "Chris, don't. Please."

She saw his hand shake slightly; he hesitated. *This is our chance,* she realized, *our last chance.*

"Chris, it's me, Liz. Look at me, please."

He turned stiffly, as if against his will. His eyes met hers and then slid away. But he didn't pick up the phone.

It was all the encouragement she needed. "Don't listen to her, Chris," Elizabeth urged. "She's planning to kill my mother like she killed Katya. It's wrong—it's evil. Don't let her make an accomplice out of you."

Chris looked at Mrs. Mueller.

"I won't tolerate this insubordination. Call the security guards, Chris," Mrs. Mueller repeated harshly, the scalpel still lifted. "Right now. Go on, do it!"

Elizabeth kept her voice soft, in contrast to Mrs. Mueller's. "You have a choice, Chris," she went on. "I know it hasn't seemed that way for a while, probably ever since you came to live at Paradise Spa, but you *do* have a choice. You don't have to obey Mrs. Mueller's orders. You can do what's right—you can help us get free."

Chris was wavering; tormented, he looked from Mrs. Mueller to Elizabeth and back again. "The choice is simple," snarled Mrs. Mueller. "Don't let her fool you, Chris. You work for me—I'm the one who takes care of you. Do as I ask."

Her words didn't have the desired impact. Chris was still immobilized, split right down the middle. *Deep down inside, he cares for me,* Elizabeth realized.

She pressed her advantage. "I know what Mrs. Mueller has put you through," she said quietly, "bringing you to Paradise and then giving you a new face and cutting you off from your old life. She treats you like you're less than human—she controls you like a robot. But you're still a human being, Chris. You're a man, with feelings and a conscience. You still have your own good judgment—that's one thing she couldn't take from you. Help us, Chris."

Chris took a step toward her. Mrs. Mueller moved quickly to counter the effect of Elizabeth's speech. "Chris, Chris," she cooed. "Don't you know this girl causes nothing but trouble? She wants to destroy our home, Chris, our family—our security, our happiness. Don't listen to her lies."

They all waited breathlessly for Chris to make a move. He remained frozen, undecided.

But someone else sprang to life. Elizabeth glimpsed a flash of color out of the corner of her eye—a girl's red shirt. It was Enid!

While Elizabeth and Mrs. Mueller had battled for Chris's heart and soul, Enid had listened in passive silence. And though Elizabeth's words hadn't been quite powerful enough to penetrate Chris's altered state, Enid had been moved by them. The spell of Paradise Spa was broken at last.

Enid leaped to Mrs. Mueller's side and snatched

the scalpel from her hand. "Let them go!" she demanded in her old, strong voice, brandishing the scalpel at Mrs. Mueller and Marguerite.

Enid's action catalyzed the boys. Releasing Jessica, Chris raced over and jumped on Mrs. Mueller, pinning her arms behind her back. Alex let go of Lila so he could overpower Marguerite.

Elizabeth's heart nearly exploded with joy and relief. She stared at Enid, her eyes shining.

Enid looked back at her, a proud smile on her face. "We're free," she said simply.

Chapter 15

A moment later four California state troopers burst into the operating theater, along with Mrs. Fowler and Lulu, the waitress and Katya's friend. Lulu, who'd recently been selected by Mrs. Mueller for training as a surgical assistant, had brought them to the remote white building by the most direct route: the secret underground passage that connected the main spa building to Mrs. Mueller's office at the clinic.

Mrs. Mueller had continued to struggle against Chris's armlock, but when she saw the police, her crooked shoulders slumped in defeat. Chris released her gently and crossed the room to where Elizabeth and Jessica were hovering over their mother.

Mrs. Wakefield was conscious but weak and confused. She tried to sit up; Elizabeth slipped an arm around her shoulders and helped her into an upright position. "Mom, are you all right?" Elizabeth asked.

Alice nodded, blinking her eyes. "I'm fine," she murmured. "Now that my girls are here, everything's fine."

Gradually, her vision cleared, and Alice gazed across the room to where a police officer was securing handcuffs around Mrs. Mueller's wrists. The two women's eyes met and held.

Sorrow and puzzlement clouded Alice's expression. She spoke softly into the silence. "Tatiana, why? How did you come to this?"

"I could never in a thousand lifetimes make you understand," Tatiana Mueller replied with a heavy sigh. "Have you not been beautiful since the day you were born? It was different for me, a misbegotten, homely child. To be so cruelly passed over when Nature was distributing her gifts! And then, as if in further punishment, to have a mother whose remarkable beauty was celebrated throughout Europe."

The prisoner sank wearily into a chair before continuing her narrative. "Ever since I was a small girl, I was obsessed with the standard of beauty that my mother personified, and devastated by the knowledge that I myself could never attain it. You recall that I told you the idea for Paradise Spa was born in my youthful tours of European spas with my mother?" Mrs. Mueller laughed bitterly. "It is true, she did allow me to tag along on her travels, but our mother-daughter bond was not as I described it.

More often than not she ignored me, but when her attention did turn my way"—Mrs. Mueller's shoulders shook; her face twisted as if she were repressing a sob—"it was only to ridicule me for my plainness in front of her glamorous friends."

Despite all the evil things Mrs. Mueller had done and conspired to do, Elizabeth couldn't help feeling a pang of pity for the miserable, love-starved child this strange woman had once been. *So she rewrote the past, creating a fantasy relationship with her mother,* Elizabeth reflected. *And maybe that's why . . .*

Enid voiced the question that had started to take shape in Elizabeth's mind. "Is that why you singled me out from the crowd?" Enid asked Mrs. Mueller. "Because you thought I needed a mother?"

Mrs. Mueller nodded. "You were alone and feeling plain, inadequate, left out. How I could relate to that! It was like stepping back in time and coming upon my younger self. I saw a chance to parent and protect you the way I never was—I had the power to shape you into someone so exquisitely beautiful, you would never again need to worry about loneliness or rejection."

She turned back to Mrs. Wakefield. "For so long I cherished my own secret hopes of transformation. Then, as a foreign student at Sweet Valley University, I encountered you, Alice Robertson, and all at once my dream came into focus. The other students had no use for ugly Tatty Mule, but they flocked eagerly around you. Every joy of life was at your fingertips!" Mrs. Mueller reminisced. "You were the golden girl, the loveliest girl in California, and then and there I vowed: Someday I would look just like you. I, too, would be proud and confident, loved and admired."

Next, Mrs. Mueller related the story, already familiar to Elizabeth, of her first failed experience with plastic surgery, her subsequent medical education, and the founding of Paradise Spa as a backdrop for Marguerite's specialized training. At that point the police prepared to take Mrs. Mueller and Marguerite into custody on charges of kidnapping, and for questioning about Katya's death and the coercive treatment of the spa's employees.

The Wakefields, Mrs. Fowler, Lila, Enid, Alex, and Chris all watched in somber silence as Mrs. Mueller took a final look around the operating theater that, happily, would never be used again. At last her eyes, sparkling with tears, settled on Alice Wakefield's face. "Farewell, my other, truer, better self," Elizabeth heard Mrs. Mueller whisper.

Late Wednesday night the Sweet Valley group got ready for bed back at Tranquillity Cottage.

It would be their last night at Paradise Spa. Having finally gotten through to Ned, who'd been on the verge of driving up to the spa, they'd told him the whole story. He offered to come get them, but since the danger was over, they decided instead to take the train home from Paradise Station the next morning.

Wearing nightgowns and robes, Elizabeth and Enid sat out on the redwood deck by the hot tub, gazing up at the peaceful night sky. A pensive silence fell over them, which Elizabeth was reluctant to break. She knew her friend had a lot to think about.

After a while Enid spoke. "This really is a beautiful place," she murmured. "It's hard to believe that under the surface so many horrible things were going on."

"You can't always judge by appearances and first impressions," Elizabeth concluded.

Enid rested her chin on her tucked-up knees. "I was really a sitting duck for Mrs. Mueller's scheming, wasn't I?" she remarked with a wry laugh. "I was feeling so sorry for myself."

"I totally understand how it happened," said Elizabeth. "She was kind to you, and so you trusted her. You had no idea what you were up against, how powerful and manipulative she'd turn out to be."

"She made me feel like she really cared about me, like she had my best interests at heart." Enid frowned. "But now that I think about it, after each time we talked, I'd feel better about her but worse about myself. I don't know how she did it. . . . I think she hypnotized me, Liz."

Elizabeth nodded. "I think that's what she did with her employees, too—people like Chris and Alex. That's how she got them to be so content with their situation here, and so intensely negative about their former lives."

"She'd start talking to me during the hair treatment or whatever, and I'd start to relax and get sleepy," Enid remembered. "And then the next thing I knew, I'd snap to, like I'd just dozed off for a minute or something. I'd always end up feeling more unhappy than ever about my looks and my life back home with Mom. But I'd also feel emptied out and relieved—I'd be grateful to Mrs. Mueller for listening, for sympathizing."

"She was planting negative memories in your brain about your mother," Elizabeth deduced. "I couldn't believe some of the things you said—you and your mom had always gotten along so well."

"I know," said Enid. She rubbed her eyes on the sleeve of her robe, blotting the tears. "I can't believe it was so easy for Mrs. Mueller to persuade me otherwise. What does that say about me? I must be a terrible person."

Elizabeth reached out to give her friend's arm a squeeze. "You're not a terrible person, you were just vulnerable. Mrs. Mueller took advantage of that. And the important thing is, you snapped out of it before it was too late."

Enid looked at Elizabeth with shining eyes. "Thanks to you," she said, sniffling. "You brought me back to reality. For days all I'd been hearing was Mrs. Mueller's voice, her suggestions, and then suddenly I heard what you were saying and I knew there was another alternative."

"You saved our lives," Elizabeth told her. "You were incredibly brave."

"I saved my own life. When I think how close I came to letting Mrs. Mueller and Marguerite operate on me!" Enid shuddered. "I would have regretted it for the rest of my life."

Elizabeth leaned over to embrace her friend. "I'm glad you didn't go through with the plastic surgery," she declared. "You're beautiful just the way you are."

Thursday morning dawned sunny and clear at Paradise Spa. Their suitcases packed, Jessica and the others walked over to the dining room for breakfast.

"Maybe there won't *be* any breakfast," remarked Lila. "I mean, without Mrs. Mueller and Marguerite here to run things, what's going to happen to this place?"

Lila's prediction was on target. They found the dining room in disorder; the tables weren't set, and the kitchen staff was wandering around aimlessly.

When Lulu and Terry saw the Sweet Valley group standing in the entrance, they hurried over. "We're just getting some fruit and yogurt and coffee ready—it'll be out in a minute," Lulu told them, running a distracted hand through her glossy cropped hair. "We didn't bake this morning—Marguerite usually writes up the menu the night before, and without it . . ."

"What will we serve for lunch?" asked Terry, chewing her lip. "And dinner?"

"Most of the guests will probably be leaving," replied Mrs. Wakefield. "You won't have to worry about us anymore . . . just about yourselves."

Lulu and Terry exchanged a startled glance. "That's right," Lulu said, a note of disbelief in her voice. "Mrs. Mueller is gone. The spa will probably shut down. We'll be on our own."

For a moment the two girls looked frightened at the prospect. Then, slowly, a smile spread across Terry's face. She repeated the key phrase. "Mrs. Mueller is gone."

Other members of the kitchen staff had gathered around, and suddenly they were all buzzing eagerly. "Mrs. Mueller is gone!" yet another voice echoed. "We don't have to work here anymore." "We can go home again!"

The mood of jubilation spread through the spa like wildfire. Within minutes the entire staff and all the guests had crowded into the dining room for a festive, informal breakfast. After placing a pitcher of fresh-squeezed orange juice on the Sweet Valley table, Lulu lingered long enough to give Mrs. Wakefield a warm hug. "After I see my own parents, I'm going to visit Katya's mother," Lulu told her. "She lives somewhere in Minnesota—last night the police told me they'd help me track her down. I want her to know what happened to Katya and that"—Lulu's eyes sparkled with tears—"that Katya loved her and missed her."

Just then Chris and Alex entered the dining room. When Alex saw Jessica, his eyes lit up; she ran across the room to throw her arms around his neck.

"You're not wearing your Paradise Spa polo shirt!" Jessica observed, touching the chest of his faded purple T-shirt with her index finger.

Alex grinned down at her. "Nope. I dug this old thing out of the bottom of my drawer—I haven't worn it in ages. It feels good, let me tell ya."

Arm in arm they strolled outside into the fragrant green courtyard. "It's like the original Independence Day in there," Jessica commented. "What are *you* going to do, now that you're free from the wicked old witch?"

"I'll be on the next train home," said Alex. "Until this morning I never really thought how worried my family must be. By now they've probably given me up for dead. Boy, will they be surprised when I walk through the door!"

"For more reasons than one," Jessica pointed out.

Alex stroked his chiseled jaw thoughtfully. "Yep. I can go home again, but I can't undo everything that happened in the past—I can't get my old face back. But, heck"—he gave her a rakishly charming smile—"it's not so bad being handsome!"

"So I guess this is good-bye."

Chris and Elizabeth were walking hand in hand

along a wooded path a stone's throw from the spa. He stopped when she spoke and turned to face her. "Yes, it is."

Chris wrapped his arms around her; Elizabeth rested her head against his broad chest. "This has been an incredible week," she murmured.

Chris stroked her hair. "Tell me about it. And to think if you and your family and friends hadn't come to Paradise, none of this would have happened—nothing would have changed. Mrs. Mueller would still be jerking us around like puppets on a string, making us into willing accomplices to her strange crimes."

Elizabeth looked up into his clear blue eyes and shook her head. "No. Sooner or later you would have come to your senses—you would have stood up for yourself."

Chris frowned. "But how long would it have taken? How many more lives might have been ruined? When I think how close I came to letting her destroy you . . ."

He bent his head in shame and remorse. Elizabeth stood on tiptoes to kiss him lightly. "All's well that end's well. I know what you had to fight against, and I'm proud of you. You didn't let me down."

Reversing direction, they headed back toward the spa where Elizabeth knew the others would be waiting for her. "Will I see you again?" Chris asked.

She had to be honest. "I don't know. I doubt it. There's . . . someone else waiting for me at home."

"Of course." He smiled ruefully. "I could have guessed that."

"But we're both writers, you and me. I'd love to get a letter from you."

"Then you will," he promised.

At the edge of the lawn they paused to look around the lush, spectacular grounds of Paradise Spa. "I should be going," Chris told Elizabeth.

She bit her lip. "Right this second? I thought we'd have a few more minutes."

Chris nodded solemnly. "Yes, because you see, although I'll be leaving Paradise, I have one last task to do before I officially quit my job as golf pro and chauffeur." He could no longer repress a mischievous grin. "I have to drive Miss Elizabeth Wakefield and party to the train station!"

Chris drove one of three vans full of departing Paradise Spa guests to the station. After loading the Sweet Valley group's luggage onto the waiting train, he gave Elizabeth one last hug.

The whistle blew, signaling that the train was about to leave the station. Jessica had already kissed Alex good-bye and now she was calling out to Elizabeth. "Hurry up, Liz, or we're going to leave you behind!"

Enid was also lingering on the platform, exchanging good-byes with Mr. and Mrs. Spencer, who were waiting for the northbound train while Randall handled the family's luggage. Just as she was about to step onto the southbound train with Elizabeth, Randall put down the last of the suitcases and ran after her. "Enid, wait!" he called.

Both Elizabeth and Enid turned. Randall was smiling up at Enid, his eyes bright with hope.

Why, he's actually handsome! Elizabeth noted with surprise. The week at the spa had done Randall a world of good; he'd lost a few pounds and gained a healthy tan.

"I wonder," Randall began shyly, "if maybe I could have your address, Enid. So we can stay in touch."

Enid was also staring dumbfounded at Randall, as if she'd never laid eyes on him before. Elizabeth nudged her in the ribs with an elbow.

"Oh, yeah, sure," Enid stammered, blushing profusely. Then she smiled. "Yeah. I'd like that."

A minute later the train was in motion. Elizabeth waved out the window at Chris; Jessica blew a kiss to Alex; Enid lifted a hand shyly to Randall. "Hey, Li, there's your boyfriend," Jessica teased, pointing to Michael, the squeaky-voiced Hollywood talent agent who was also standing on the platform waiting for the next train. "Aren't you going to wave good-bye?"

Lila scowled. "How would you like a little spontaneous plastic surgery?" she countered, reaching over to give Jessica's bare arm a pinch.

The train picked up speed, the wooded landscape passing in a green blur. Elizabeth settled back in her seat and gazed at her mother. "I've never been so happy to be going home in my entire life," she said. "Sometimes in the past I've taken you and Dad for granted, Mom, but never again!"

"We're lucky to have each other," Mrs. Wakefield agreed.

Elizabeth was pensive for a moment. "Mrs. Mueller was really twisted, wasn't she?" she observed at last. "She picked you out of the crowd at Sweet Valley University all those years ago, but she never saw that it wasn't just your looks that made you popular and happy. She thought if she had a pretty face, everything would be easy for her."

"It doesn't necessarily work that way," remarked Mrs. Fowler.

"It's what's inside that counts," Enid contributed.

Mrs. Wakefield sighed. "And inside, Tatiana was a sick and bitter woman. You know, if she ever *had* had plastic surgery, if she had become beautiful, it would have been a harsh awakening. She would have discovered that she still carried around her misery and resentment in her heart and mind."

"But some stuff about Paradise Spa was great," Jessica put in. "Admit it—at the beginning we all loved it. We loved being pampered and beautified."

"Sure," admitted Mrs. Wakefield. "It's just a question of keeping things in perspective, of not forgetting what's really important in life." She took Jessica's hand and gave it a squeeze. "Like family relationships based on love and trust."

"Mrs. Mueller thought she'd created a family at Paradise Spa, but in her own way she behaved just as badly to her 'children' as the real parents they ran away from," said Elizabeth. "She exploited their insecurities and abused her power."

"A parent should build up a child from the inside out, not the other way around," Mrs. Fowler concluded.

One by one they leaned back in their seats to enjoy the ride. Jessica and Lila pulled out fashion magazines; Enid made a trip to the dining car for diet sodas; Grace and Alice opened their novels.

Unzipping her computer carrying case, Elizabeth opened her laptop. Logging on, she typed in Todd's E-mail address. All at once she couldn't wait to see him again and tell him everything about her vacation at Paradise Spa. Well—she remembered Chris's tender good-bye kiss and blushed—*almost* everything.

"Hi, Todd. Guess what? We're coming home a few days early," Elizabeth wrote. "And boy, do I have a story for you!"

Don't miss SVH #115, **The Treasure of Death Valley**, *the first book in the next riveting two-part miniseries.*

Bantam Books in the Sweet Valley High series
Ask your bookseller for the books you have missed

#1 DOUBLE LOVE
#2 SECRETS
#3 PLAYING WITH FIRE
#4 POWER PLAY
#5 ALL NIGHT LONG
#6 DANGEROUS LOVE
#7 DEAR SISTER
#8 HEARTBREAKER
#9 RACING HEARTS
#10 WRONG KIND OF GIRL
#11 TOO GOOD TO BE TRUE
#12 WHEN LOVE DIES
#13 KIDNAPPED!
#14 DECEPTIONS
#15 PROMISES
#16 RAGS TO RICHES
#17 LOVE LETTERS
#18 HEAD OVER HEELS
#19 SHOWDOWN
#20 CRASH LANDING!
#21 RUNAWAY
#22 TOO MUCH IN LOVE
#23 SAY GOODBYE
#24 MEMORIES
#25 NOWHERE TO RUN
#26 HOSTAGE
#27 LOVESTRUCK
#28 ALONE IN THE CROWD
#29 BITTER RIVALS
#30 JEALOUS LIES
#31 TAKING SIDES
#32 THE NEW JESSICA
#33 STARTING OVER
#34 FORBIDDEN LOVE
#35 OUT OF CONTROL
#36 LAST CHANCE
#37 RUMORS
#38 LEAVING HOME
#39 SECRET ADMIRER
#40 ON THE EDGE
#41 OUTCAST
#42 CAUGHT IN THE MIDDLE
#43 HARD CHOICES
#44 PRETENSES
#45 FAMILY SECRETS
#46 DECISIONS
#47 TROUBLEMAKER
#48 SLAM BOOK FEVER
#49 PLAYING FOR KEEPS
#50 OUT OF REACH
#51 AGAINST THE ODDS
#52 WHITE LIES
#53 SECOND CHANCE
#54 TWO-BOY WEEKEND
#55 PERFECT SHOT
#56 LOST AT SEA
#57 TEACHER CRUSH
#58 BROKENHEARTED
#59 IN LOVE AGAIN
#60 THAT FATAL NIGHT
#61 BOY TROUBLE
#62 WHO'S WHO?
#63 THE NEW ELIZABETH
#64 THE GHOST OF TRICIA MARTIN
#65 TROUBLE AT HOME
#66 WHO'S TO BLAME?
#67 THE PARENT PLOT
#68 THE LOVE BET
#69 FRIEND AGAINST FRIEND
#70 MS. QUARTERBACK
#71 STARRING JESSICA!
#72 ROCK STAR'S GIRL
#73 REGINA'S LEGACY
#74 THE PERFECT GIRL
#75 AMY'S TRUE LOVE
#76 MISS TEEN SWEET VALLEY
#77 CHEATING TO WIN
#78 THE DATING GAME
#79 THE LONG-LOST BROTHER

#80 THE GIRL THEY BOTH LOVED
#81 ROSA'S LIE
#82 KIDNAPPED BY THE CULT!
#83 STEVEN'S BRIDE
#84 THE STOLEN DIARY
#85 SOAP STAR
#86 JESSICA AGAINST BRUCE
#87 MY BEST FRIEND'S BOYFRIEND
#88 LOVE LETTERS FOR SALE
#89 ELIZABETH BETRAYED
#90 DON'T GO HOME WITH JOHN
#91 IN LOVE WITH A PRINCE
#92 SHE'S NOT WHAT SHE SEEMS
#93 STEPSISTERS
#94 ARE WE IN LOVE?
#95 THE MORNING AFTER
#96 THE ARREST
#97 THE VERDICT
#98 THE WEDDING
#99 BEWARE THE BABY-SITTER
#100 THE EVIL TWIN (MAGNA)
#101 THE BOYFRIEND WAR
#102 ALMOST MARRIED
#103 OPERATION LOVE MATCH
#104 LOVE AND DEATH IN LONDON
#105 A DATE WITH A WEREWOLF
#106 BEWARE THE WOLFMAN (SUPER THRILLER)
#107 JESSICA'S SECRET LOVE
#108 LEFT AT THE ALTAR
#109 DOUBLE-CROSSED
#110 DEATH THREAT
#111 A DEADLY CHRISTMAS (SUPER THRILLER)
#112 JESSICA QUITS THE SQUAD
#113 THE POM-POM WARS
#114 "V" FOR VICTORY

SUPER EDITIONS:
PERFECT SUMMER
SPECIAL CHRISTMAS
SPRING BREAK
MALIBU SUMMER
WINTER CARNIVAL
SPRING FEVER

SUPER STARS:
LILA'S STORY
BRUCE'S STORY
ENID'S STORY
OLIVIA'S STORY
TODD'S STORY

SUPER THRILLERS:
DOUBLE JEOPARDY
ON THE RUN
NO PLACE TO HIDE
DEADLY SUMMER
MURDER ON THE LINE
BEWARE THE WOLFMAN
A DEADLY CHRISTMAS
MURDER IN PARADISE

MAGNA EDITIONS:
THE WAKEFIELDS OF SWEET VALLEY
THE WAKEFIELD LEGACY: THE UNTOLD STORY
A NIGHT TO REMEMBER
THE EVIL TWIN
ELIZABETH'S SECRET DIARY
JESSICA'S SECRET DIARY